MO' MONEY MO' PROBLEMS

THE COME-UP

MO' MONEY MO' PROBLEMS

This book is a work of fiction. Any resemblance to names, characters, or incidents are purely coincidental.

ISBN 978-0-578-19082-2

Acknowledgments

First I have to give all praises to The Almighty GOD because with him I couldn't have made it this far in life!

I did this for my Mama, Denise, My brothers Kenny and Joe, My sisters Cammi and Everettca, My nephew Tre, My Neices Erin and Riley and My son Corey L. Jackson Jr. and his mother, Nette.

WE GOT US IF NOBODY ELSE DO!

My day ones Dennis, Will, James and Dee, Yall know what it is!

To all my Aunts, Uncles and Cousins, I love yall so much and appreciate everyone of you. To any feeling lost or trapped in the struggle, NEVER stop believing or grinding, Better days are for coming!

ANYTHING IS POSSIBLE!

MMMP

*TO MY GRANNY OLLIE AND BESTFRIEND GIZZLE,
FLY HIGH MY ANGELS.*

THE COME-UP

Chapter1

It was the spring of '04 as I walked across the stage. "Congratulations Mr. Logan."

"Thanks," I said, as I looked into the auditorium full of parents who were glad to see their "wanna be" grown kids graduating high school. It seems like just yesterday I was a scrawny little freshman looking forward to making the basketball team, but now my entire school career was quickly becoming a memory.

After graduation, me and a few of my classmates hopped into one of my friends we called "Big T" Lasabre', we were going as far away from school as possible! Juicy and Slink were talking about some college shit as I drove and T rolled up a blunt. "Where y'all see us in five years?" asked Slink, who was always going off the deep end when we got high. It was a question we had been asked a lot recently and all throughout our senior year, but personally I never gave it much thought. I told him we wasn't tryna hear that shit right now and turned up the

Boosie & Webbie on his ass. Truth be told, the only thing I've thought about lately was hanging around the projects with my lil bro, getting fucked up and tryna sell enough of this weed to make my money back. I was smart, hell I had just finished high school in 3 ½ years, but that wasn't putting any paper in my pocket. It probably would in the future but in the hood the future wasn't thought about like that. So, my mission was to get paid now! I saw how all the big homies was riding around on spinning rims and all the hoes was on them. I definitely wanted some of that. I had a little weed for sale but I had a big smoking habit and an obsession for the new J's. Not to mention, I had three brothers and sisters who were all younger than me, so of course I looked out for them when I could. I never tripped on spending the lil money I had because I knew that one day I would be a baller and money wouldn't be a problem. Little did I know, B.I.G. wasn't lying when he said, "Mo money, Mo problems. "

CHAPTER 2

As the summer started, I kind of lost contact with my homies from school. I had been hanging out with my lil bro JG and my nigga from the apartments named Tugg. Like myself, Tugg had just graduated and had the same goal I had in mind so we got real cool throughout the summer. Every day, we would smoke, and at night we would come up with some money for a pint of Remy. Me and JG would go to the boys and girls club to hoop for most of the day, then it would be straight to the apartments. One hot ass day in July I walked in my mama's house and an older man was sitting on the couch with her. She told me to sit down and the man introduced himself as an Army recruiter. I chuckled a little and looked at her like "What the fuck he here for?". He went on to ask me several type of questions about different types of things. Most subjects that I had never thought about but one subject in particular I had been asked a lot lately, "Where do you see yourself five years from now?". Here I was, high-as-a -kite, eyes bloodshot red from the dro, sitting on my mama's couch thinking, "You've got to be kidding me." I told him, "I don't see myself in the Army." My mama looked completely disappointed while the recruiter packed up his computer and other belongings. As he shook my hand, he told me to think about my future, gave me his card and told me to call him if I ever changed my mind. As me and moms sat there, she was highly agitated about my demeanor and low level of concern for my future. She said "Darius you grown now and I can't have you here not doing shit! You aren't trying go to college nor do you have a job! You gone have to do something with your life instead of getting high all the damn time!"

"Aight ma," I said as I left out, headed to the apartments to hang with my click. Uncle Sam didn't stand a chance recruiting me; I was headed to the streets to be all I can be! Later on that night we were riding in Tugg's Taurus getting drunk. We all started talking about how we was gone get some money and come up. In Tugg's lap sat an old revolver that his grandfather had given him. He suggested that we become stick-up kids. Lil bro's idea was to start selling fake dope. I just sat back listening to them go on and on, with these damn near crazy ideas that didn't sound right to me. I had drifted into another world thinking about my girl Susie who I had been fucking with for a lil while now. Although she was a year younger than me she had been my rider since we meet and she had seen me go from nothing, to a tennis-shoe hustler. I loved her though because she was real and her mom was cool as fuck. It was nothing for me to go and spend the night with them on any given night. "Nigga, snap out of it!" JG spat at me, as he nudged my arm with the Remy. He knew me better than anybody else because we had been through a lot together as "youngster's." "She aint going nowhere bro!"."Y'all niggas trippin," I said. "We tryna figure out how we gone get some money out here and all y'all coming up with is quick ways to get us killed for nothing. I would run in a bank before I rob any of these broke ass niggas out here or sell some fake dope. Matter of fact, drop me off at my girl house." I was irritated by the day's events and the liquor and dro had me horny as fuck. I had to get away from these niggas!

CHAPTER 3

As we pulled up to Susie's crib, I called to tell her to come open the door. I shook up with my niggas gave them a couple blunts and told them to be careful. Susie opened the door to the two-story double in boy shorts and a beater. She had a small frame, bite sized titties and a nice ass for her petite frame. As she turned away to head back to her room the liquor and dro mixed with the sight of her sexy, bare legs had me ready to release some of this built-up frustration on her. I smacked that ass as she led me upstairs to her room. Feeling that ass jiggle got me more excited! She playfully smacked my hand away and told me to "roll up." I said, "Damn, I aint bring no swishers." She went to her mom's room and brought back a big boy philly. I passed her the sack and told her to get tight. As she licked the philly to split it open, she caught me in a daze. "Baby, what's wrong with you?" she asked. With the liquor getting the best of me, I started venting about my day with the recruiter and how moms was tripping. "I need to get some real money baby," I said. "Stop buying all them shoes and smoking so much and start saving, then you a probably have more" she said. "Not you too," I replied. "Not me what? I'm just being honest baby, you smoke all day and you buy a new pair of shoes almost every week," she said as she passed me the blunt. "I aint tryna sound like yo mama or nothing because I accept you as is, but you complaining about being broke when you really choosing to be broke." As she talked I just sat back smoking. I wasn't tryna hear the shit she was saying because in my head the money I spent on shoes and smoked up every day wasn't the type of money I was referring to when I said money. It was becoming obvious to me that my definition and broke and the mufuckas around me definition of it was two different things. As we continued to make small talk she got up, put on a slow mix and straddled me. "Don't worry about all that shit baby. This our time," she said as she pulled my shirt over my head and unbuttoned my Girbauds. She pulled my dick out and sucked away all the stress I had. After busting that first nut we both got naked and fucked till we passed out. I liked sleeping over her house because her mom's worked late night until about 8 in the morning and she didn't trip on us smoking in her house. I could get a good night's rest, fire sex and wake up and get high without having to go anywhere..."BOOM, BOOM, BOOM" The next morning we woke up to banging on the door. "Son-in-law, get up and go to the VP to get me a swisher and lemon juice," her mom's yelled. I had no problem getting up after the rendezvous last night. Me and her brother Q got dressed and headed to the gas station on the corner. Her brother Q was a lil younger than me but he was cool nigga. He said he had to meet somebody on the next street over, so we bounced. While we were walking, he told me he met one of his customers every morning around the same spot. "What you be selling?" I asked him. "Crack, but don't tell Susie because I don't want mom to find out," he said. "I got you, I got you but who the fuck put yo little ass on?" I asked truly interested. "My nigga at school, he stealing it from his big brother and giving me a couple grams every now and then" he stated. "Oh," was all I could say, as we approached the abandoned house. In front of it sat a Lexus truck. Q told me to watch his back as he went to the driver's side to serve the older man in the suit. He looked old enough to be either one of our fathers. "D, come here," Q hollered from where he was standing.

"What up lil bro?"

"Can I give him your number? He said he wanna holla at me a lil later but I aint got no phone."

"Yeah" I said, as I spat my number to the old school. As we walked back towards the gas station, lil Q showed me a gospel cassette the man had passed him with forty dollars in it. "You just made $40 dollars off him?" I asked in disbelief. "Yeah," he said, "and that's every day. He a preacher but he get high."

"What the fuck?" I said, more to myself but out loud. Now my mind was going crazy, I don't know if I was more shocked at the preacher getting high or the lil nigga having this sweet ass play. I walked back to his house after we grabbed the swishers mostly in silence, listening to him tell me that grams go for $25 but you can make almost $150 off it. After we got back to their house, Me and Susie smoked with her mom and after that I called Tugg to come pick me up.

CHAPTER 4

"Where JG at?" I asked Tugg as I hopped into the passenger side.

"I aint hollered at him today. Last night after we dropped you off, he had me take him to the apartments," he said. JG and Tugg were really cool through me. They never really hung out together unless I was with them. "So, what's up for today?" I asked. "You know Boosie has a concert tomorrow," he said, "you tryna hit the mall and get something to wear?" "Yeah but I gotta get some more weed first, so drop me off in the apartments and we a link up later.

"Aight, bet," Tugg said as he pulled off.

After he dropped me off I got a couple ounces of weed, bagged up some sacks and put some up. I was out there with JJ and Nic, a couple younger dudes from around the way, when Tugg pulled up. "What up bro," I yelled.

"What's up nigga you ready to hit the mall?"

"Yeah," I said. JJ and Nic said they wanted to ride with us so we all cut out. "Let's go put up the gun," I told Tugg as we were leaving the apartments. I wasn't a big fan of riding around four deep with a gun for no reason. "Naw let me hold it" Nic hollered from the backseat. Tugg gave it to him and we was out. As we were getting high listening to "Swerve," no one noticed the cruiser behind us until it was too late. "Aw shit, everybody be cool the boys behind us," Tugg said. As if they didn't believe him, JJ and Nic both looked back which caused the officer to hit the lights and sirens. 'THUMP THUMP" I felt something hit the driver's seat. I looked down to see it was the revolver. Tugg had already pulled over and put the car in park, so I told him to hurry up and slide the gun under the seat. He did it as the cop approached the window.

"License and registration please," the officer says. Tugg passed him his L's and reaches in the glove compartment to grab the registration. The officer asked everyone in the car for their ID and only Tugg and myself had any type of ID on us. So, the officer called for backup and they arrived immediately. As we were escorted from the car and placed in restraints, the officers ordered us to sit on the curb until he conducted a search. I was furious and it showed on my face. I was scared to look up and everybody was acting like wasn't nothing in the car until the officer said, "Look what we got here, who's is this?" Everything went completely silent. "Okay, if no one wants to speak up everybody is going down." Just what the fuck I needed, I thought to myself. After the police ran everybody's name and realized that only Tugg and I were 18, he decided to put the gun on us. Nic had two warrants and JJ was free to go. In the wagon I was fuming and calling Nic every bitch in the book. If we weren't separated by the metal in the back I would of beat the fuck out of dude. He didn't say one word as Tugg and I were going to jail and he was going to the juvenile hall. After sitting in processing for what seemed like forever, but was really only 12 hours, we were both released on our own recognizance and the case was sealed for a year. Neither of us had records. The judge said as long as we stayed out of trouble we would be cool, but that the state could refile charges within 365 days.

By time I made it to my mama's house it was near midnight. I took a shower, turned on B.E.T. and dozed off. The next day I went to the apartments to meet Tugg, just like we did every day. As I walked, I was on the phone with Susie listening to her tell me to stay out them apartments cause nothing good was going for me hanging out there. As I crossed the field, I saw none other than JJ and Nic sitting on the green-box. I walked past them mugging hard as fuck, but listening to Susie I kept going about my way. As I made it to Tugg's spot, we rolled up a couple blunts and went to pick up two chicks from the housing complex down the street. When I saw JJ and Nic bend the corner I knew what time it was. I told Tugg, "Make sure they don't jump me," and hopped out ready for whatever. As if on que, JJ flicked the butt off his cigarette at my feet and I immediately cracked him in the face. As he stumbled, I turned towards Nic and got to pouncing on him. In the meantime, JJ got back to his feet and rushed me, He tackled me to the ground and then started hitting me on top of my head. I managed to grab his fist and yelled at him, "bitch let me up and I'm a beat yo ass, hoe ass nigga." Tugg was holding Nic back, preventing them from jumping me. JJ got off me, got up, and they both ran. I was livid, by now a crowd had appeared and I was shirtless telling them niggas lets go toe-to-toe, heads up, but they were gone. As I got back in the ride, the chicks were snickering a little and I heard one of them said, "you got yo ass beat." "Drop these sack chasing sluts off," I told Tugg. He rolled up a blunt and we passed it back and forth as we rode to the complex where the chicks stayed. We dropped them off, and I told Tugg to take me to my mama's crib. I'd catch up with him tomorrow I was irritated.

The next day I woke up, I had several missed calls from an unknown number. When I called the number back, a man answered after three rings and said "hello."

I said, "what up somebody call me?"

"yeah," the caller said on the other end. "I'm tryna hook up with you, I got 50"

"What? Who the fuck is this?"

"Oh, I'm looking for Q."

"Q? Oh yeah, Q. You said you got 50?"

Yeah," he said.

"Where you want me to come to?"

"Meet me at 30th and Tacoma."

"How long you gone be?" I asked.

"Bout a half hour".

"Aight call when you get close."

I had no one I fucked with heavily to buy some dope from, so I called JG. "What up big bro, why aint you hollered at me in a few days?" He said.

"I been beefing with them niggas in the apartments but fuck that where you at, I need to holler at you."

"Aight meet me at mama's house," I said before we hung up. He was there in no time. "Lil bro, I need a gram of hard who you know that a sell me one?" I asked him. He looked at me puzzled and said, "When you start selling dope?" I told him I had somebody who had $50 and he stopped all the questions. He told me his big brother Moe who had just got sent to the joint, has a best friend named Peewee who lived nearby and could hook us up. "Cool," I said. We called Peewee and he brought it to us within 15 minutes. We sat on my broke down Honda, rolling up a blunt and examining this gram of crack. "Don't touch it and then touch the blunt with the same fingers," he said. He showed me how to break it down into smaller pieces and told me to try to give the customer just enough to satisfy him. We were interrupted by a phone ring. "Hello," I quickly answered. "I'm pulling up," the caller said. "Okay, park and I'll be over there in a minute." I walked over to him and was surprised at the small amount he took for the crispy $50. "Is it cool if I call you from now on?" he asked. "Sure," I said, "what's your name so I can program you in my phone?" "Just call me Preacher Man," he said. His eyes were looking at the rock like they were going to pop out his head. As I made it back around the corner with JG, I was turned up. I already doubled my money and still had more than half of the product left, it would've took me hours to make 50 off the weed round here, I thought to myself. As I approached JG I was all smiles, "I think I found our come up lil bro!" As the summer went by I started to focus on my grind and spending more time with my girl. I started grabbing a quarter pound of weed every week and was keeping a gram of hard for when Preacher Man called. By September when school started, I brought my two sisters and lil brother school supplies and a pair of shoes. Susie dropped out of school but I still bought her some gear and I bought myself a nice chain with a bracelet attached and a cross charm on it. My birthday was the weekend of the Circle City Classic and I had huge plans on enjoying the whole weekend. Tugg, JG and I went to Lafayette Square Mall and were having a ball. Shit was finally looking better for a nigga. I bought me and JG some Barkley's and jerseys and Tugg bought some Forces. When we left the mall, I told him to stop by mama's so I can drop this shit off. When I went into the house my mama was in the living room, "Darius come here," she said. I walked into the room high as hell and said "what's up ma?" She handed me a key and told me she got me and my cousin Maria an apartment on the other side of town. Maria was a couple years older than me and had a newborn. I was dumb founded for some reason. She said, "Aint no room for you here no more, I told you I gotta take care of your brothers and sisters. I gave you all summer to get your shit together. I got you an apartment, paid your half of the first month's rent. Now you're on your own baby." I felt kind of abandoned but I wouldn't let her see it so I took the key, put my shit from the mall up and left her crib. I aint tell my niggas what happened, because I didn't realize the seriousness of it at the time. So, we went on about our normal routine. As the weekend came we partied hard. We smoked, drank, and even popped x-pills for the first time. Sunday night, we rode down 38th street following traffic, getting high as usual. I turned the radio down and told them I would be moving out the inner city to the eastside and told them how my moms got me a crib setup. "Well I aint got no gas money to be coming out there every day getting yo ass," Tugg said sarcastically but meaning it. JG just sat back wondering how this was gone work. That night the three of us made a pack that we would all get on the grind for real, get our shit together and hook-up soon. Shortly after that, I had Tugg drop me off at Susie's. I called her when I got to the door, she opened it and we went upstairs to her room where she had *Love and Basketball* playing. I rolled up a blunt and it kicked my x-pill back into effect. I started kissing on her while I felt on that pussy through the shit she had on. I kissed her from her hips down to her navel ring before pulling her shorts down and sucking on her clit till she started trembling, I slid my pant and boxers off turned her over and tried to stick my dick as far as it would reach in her. After pounding her for hours she passed out in my arms. I lay there wondering how it was going to be being so far away from my daily routine and in foreign land. I went to school with a lot of people from the Far East but I had never actually been out there like that. Now I would be living out there. My weed customers were mostly from the apartments and had no transportation. Even if they did they wouldn't come way out there for a sack when it was 10 more weed-men in the area. Preacher Man was calling less and less lately so I felt like I was starting from scratch again. All I had was some weed, close to $1000 and my ambition.

Chapter 6

Adapting to new environments was naturally easy for me, although I was born in Indianapolis, I lived in Greenville, SC for a few years as a kid. We moved back to "Naptown" in the late ninety's. I went to five different junior high schools before moms got comfortable in the house across from the apartments Tugg and I hung out in. I was no stranger to being the new guy. The Far East side was like a city within a city. More than 20 apartment complexes surrounded by housing communities, gas stations and liquor stores on every corner. Being a project raised baby, I felt right at home. The fall of 2004 was in full fledge and my cousin and I were getting used to our new crib. We had a couple more cousins who stayed in some of the surrounding apartments and every day I was seeing different people I knew from school. I still had some bud for sale and I made sure kept my phone on at all times. I would walk to the gas stations nearly ten times a day with a pocket of dimes and twenty bags. I began passing my number out to people I knew and to people who bought sacks from me. Word of mouth was spreading and my phone was ringing. I was easily starting to sell all my weed in a matter of 2-3 days and beginning to like my new surroundings. As Thanksgiving and Christmas came around my grind was elevating. I hadn't been talking to JG, Tugg or Susie lately but every now and then I would call and check up on them. I didn't have time to be playing phone tag because I had bills to pay and I was becoming a man overnight. By spring of 2005 my grind had done a whole 360. I had bought me a '91 Buick and tinted it out. I had close to 5 Gs saved, my license, gun permit and a bubble Chevy waiting to be rimmed up. Once I got my Buick out the tint shop, I called JG and Tugg and told them I was coming to pick them up. As we rode down 38th street we were all excited about being together again. We began to roll up and start reminiscing and shit. "I told yall we was gone hook up again," I said as we headed east on 38th Street. " I don't know what yall did over the winter but I did what I said I was gone do!" I pulled out a fat ass 9mm Taurus I copped and told them how I was getting my shit together. JG seemed excited for me but I could feel the jealousy coming from T as he said, "bout time nigga." We continued to ride out East joking and clowning till we pulled up to my complex. Neither of them had been over here before, so they aint know this was my crib. "Come on, we can chill in my shit," I said. "Where cuz at?" JG asked. "She take the baby and go chill with her baby daddy every weekend," I told them. "So you be having the spot all to yourself?" Tugg asked. "Yea nigga, this my shit!" I arrogantly replied. My phone rang and I had a couple people to meet so I told them "let's go." We went to serve a few of my people and by the time we looked up it was night-time. "Let's hit the L," JG said. I pulled up to the liquor store and told them all drinks was on me. I grabbed a fifth of Goose and a box of Swishers. We went back to my house and got wasted as they caught me up with what was going on in the city. JG had been on the west-end selling dope and Tugg had a job at Kroger's, A local grocery store. He was also selling weed in the apartments. It felt good to be back with my niggas getting drunk like we use to. After that night, JG stayed out east with me and we became inseparable like before. We would stay out all night meeting our people, pulling up at gas stations, flirting with hoes anywhere we could catch them at and looking for new customers. One day as were at the hottest gas station on the east side we were flagged down by a couple chicks I knew from school. Krissy and

Andrea. "Yall tryna buy some weed?" I asked them after seeing the swishers in their hand. "Naw we got some," but we'll match yall if that's cool?" Andrea replied.

"Aight hop in, where we going?" I asked. "I stay down the street, we can go over my house," she told us. They hopped in and gave us directions of where to go. Ironically, she stayed in the same complex I stayed in, but in the next court. We went inside to smoke, and we talked about how we use to skip school back in the days to do the same thing. They invited us over for dinner the upcoming Friday. I told her we would be there and we exchanged numbers and we dipped. Later on that night before heading in, we caught a potential customer on a pay phone. "Look bro, its four in the morning, what you think he doing on a pay phone?" I asked lil bro as I turned in the Citgo lot. I pulled up next to him let the window down and asked him what's up?

"What's up with yall?" he said. "Yall working?"

"Yeah," I said, "follow us." He hung up, hopped in his car and followed us to my apartment. As we parked I signaled for him to get in the back. We made him hit the blunt to be sure he wasn't the law and he hit it so hard he had it dragging. "What's yo name?" I asked.

"Larry," he said.

"What you looking for?"

"I got 40. I need 30 hard and 10 green," he went on to say. I served him the green and bro served him the hard. As we continued to smoke the blunt he told us that he had a bunch of family and friends that got high and he was willing to hook us up with them if we were always on.

"Hell yea, we always on," I said. I wrote down my number for him. He took the number with promises to be in touch with us soon. As the days passed Larry became a regular, some days he was calling 4-5 times and he had his mama, brothers & sisters, nephews and friends calling. Money was coming but I was missing most of it because I didn't have the work. One day while JG and I were riding, we pulled up on Peewee. We stayed at his spot for a minute, smoking and playing X-Box. Peewee was a real d-boy. His door never stopped while we were there and his customers didn't all look like junkies like Larry did. I asked him how much he would sell me for a hundred and he told me 4 grams. He sat down with me and JG and broke the game all the way down to us from a kilo to a gram and explained to us how to turn the powder to hard and the different process and profits. Although he was only a year older than me, he was much more advanced in the dope game. He told us how he and Big Moe had been selling dope since they were 11 and 12 and how much he learned from the dope game. He told me he could see that ambition in me and gave me his number and told me to come hang out with him sometimes. After smoking a box of blunts and playing Madden for hours, I took my 4 grams and JG and I headed back to my spot. I like Peewee, I told JG. "Yeah, he a cool nigga," he replied. "But what's up with them hoes? Ol girl and her buddy aint never call you?"

"Naw let me call them." After a couple of rings a female picked up. "Hello," she said.

"What up, is this Andrea?" I asked.

"Yea what's up Darius?"

"Shit, wondering what happened to that dinner yall promised us."

"We kinda got tied up but what yall doing now?" she asked.

"We tryna come chill with yall, we got some smoke."

"ok, come through," she said. Me and JG made our way over her house but stopped and grabbed some L and blunts first. After drinking and smoking, she ended up telling us that she had to give her mama most of her food stamps so they didn't really have any extra money to spend. I quickly volunteered to go to the store. Me and Andrea went to the local grocery store and she bought hot wings and shit to make spaghetti. We made small talk and were realizing we had more in common that we knew we had. After she finished cooking it was a little late and everybody was full, drunk and high. Krissy asked if I could drop her off and I agreed but told Andrea she would have to ride with me because JG wanted to get dropped off in the city. After dropping both of them off we rode back to our apartments and I was surprised to see that after all the liquor and weed, she was still wide awoke and alert. "Can you roll-up while I drive?" I asked her. She said, "where it's at?" I gave her the weed and told her the swishers were in the middle console. She twisted it up without dropping any on my floor. As we continued to make small talk I was becoming more attracted to her. When we got in front of her building I asked if I could come back in and she said "I knew you was gone say that, but come on.'" When we got upstairs we got to kissing on each other and she told me I wasn't ready for a woman like her as she stripped down to her G-string. I got naked and she asked me if I had a condom. I pulled it out, opened it and put it on. She got on all fours and told me to hit it from the back. As I entered her wetness, I was in awe of how that pussy felt. Unlike Susie, she was a thick stallion with a fat ass and long jet black hair. I hit her from the back before she turned over and hopped on top showing me she like to be in control. This was by far the best sex I've ever had; I was starting to feel like the boss I was born to be. After we were done I got up, got dressed and was getting ready to leave until I heard her smack her teeth or something. I started complexing like, I aint just put it down on her or something. I wasn't the biggest but I definitely wasn't slacking so I asked her, "What's wrong with you?"

"I knew you was gone try to fuck me and leave like I'm a little girl or something." She snapped back. What the fuck... I thought to myself as I stared at her lost for words. "What?" was all I could say, I had fucked many chicks but Susie was the only chick I ever actually spent a night with. That just wasn't my M.O. I was at a crossroads because I knew she was the clingy type and if I choose to spend a night this would be the beginning of a mind game women play. She gave me that puppy dog look and said, "Where you got to go this late anyway?" I aint have an answer for her. I thought to myself, fuck it. Why not lay up in this good ass pussy for a night?

Chapter 7

Summer time was here and being broke was a thing of the past for me! I had over 10 bands stacked away and was living the high life. I started looking out for moms lately and it felt good to do that. Drea and I had started kicking it heavy and I started keeping some drugs at her apartment. She had become my down-ass-chic. She never asked for much, kept my stomach full and was down for whatever, whenever I needed her. Me, JG and Tugg had started going to under 21 clubs where we stood out because of our swag. The bitches were choosing us and the niggas hated us. One night me and JG were in the club and Juvenile's "Slow Motion" was blasting through the speakers. I noticed a few niggas mugging in our direction as we were hugged up with a couple chicks. I got JGs attention and motioned with my eyes and a head nod for him to look over there. They were quickly headed our way. We were outnumbered but backing down wasn't an option. As they surrounded us, one of the dudes who had dreads and glasses, grabbed the arm of the girl I was with, she didn't try to break from his grip so I figured she must have known him. With that said, the x-pill I had popped before the club had my ego shattered a little so I attempted to grab her back but was quickly blindsided by one of their homeboys. That started a mini rumble. JG hit the dude that hit me directly in the mouth with a right jab and caught another one with a left hook. I was on dread heads top, when I felt somebody trying to grab my neck. Bitches got to fighting in another section and security started spraying mace in the air. As I spotted my charm on the ground I was trying to locate my chain but it was clearly lost in the crowd. JG grabbed me and we headed to the parking lot. Outside the club seemed more packed than the inside. You could feel the tension in the air. We were blocked in so we couldn't leave if we wanted too. I saw JG go to the passenger side of the whip and I immediately knew he was grabbing the heat. As he came back to where I was he said, "Bro, let these niggas play crazy if they want too! Somebody mama gone cry tonight!" The look in bro eyes let me know shit was about to get real. As the whole parking lot's attention turned to a couple hoes yelling at the top of their lungs, I noticed shorty I was on in the club and made my way to her to holler at her. "What up ma, you good?" I asked.

"Yeah, that was my brother and his friends being overprotective, I'm sorry," she said.

"You aint got shit to be sorry for," I told her as I reached for her hand. "What's your name?"

"Tori," she said.

"Can I call you?" I asked. She gave me her number in the midst of all the drama that was going on and I turned to go back where JG was. As I made my way through the crowd I spotted the niggas we had just fought and one of them had my chain on, "Brooo!" I called out to JG, he looked at me and seen I was headed in the direction where the niggas was. I walked right up on dude and snatched my shit off homies neck and his boys was starting to rush me till JG pulled out the heat and said, "Any one of you niggas take another step and one of these niggas gone be rushing you to the ER!" They must though it was a game cause next thing I know, I saw sparks flying toward them niggas as they rushed us, "BOC, BOC, BOC, BOC" I saw a body drop and all hell broke loose, more shots were let off from a distance and people were hopping in their cars and pulling off. "Bro come on!" I yelled and we hopped in my ride and peeled out. I heard screaming and seen 2 bodies sprawled out in the parking lot as we made our exit. Our adrenaline was pumping as we headed out east. I had to calm my nerves so I could do the speed limit without getting pulled over. I looked over at bro and he was calm as ever like nothing happened. That's what I like about this nigga. His demeanor never changed but deep down we both knew it may be consequences for this. It was nearly 100 witnesses out there and everybody know; loose lips sink ships.

Chapter 8

We laid low for a while and I was nervous as hell but that didn't stop me from getting my money. It did stop me from hitting the malls and going out for a while. Our lease was up and my cousin didn't want to renew it, so I moved in with Drea and was just staying off the scene. I was becoming very comfortable around her and my stash was getting fat as hell. Our relationship was very open. As long as I was home every night she aint really trip on me. I had it made. As summer was coming to an end Me, Tugg and JG had plans to go to Cincinnati for the weekend to party and shop a lil bit.

We was in the '06 Dodge Charger rental that moms got for me reminiscing about how much shit had changed since last summer. Me and JG had been together damn near every day, so we were mostly listening to Tugg tell us how he had a baby on the way and how the weed game wasn't doing shit for him. "Sound like you stressing my nigga," I said as I passed the blunt to JG.

"Yeah I'm fucked up, plus my lil cuz got killed a couple months ago and that's fucking my mind up because he was just here for the summer and was supposed to be starting his Sophomore year at the University of Tennessee this fall. His moms blaming me cause he was supposed to be staying with us at my Pop's crib but he chose to go out with his hood niggas to club holla and ended up getting murked,"

"You talking about the under 21 club? JG asked.

"Yea, remember hearing bout two murders last month?" he said. "Yeah," we both said in unison.

"That was my lil cousin," he said sadly. JG and I gave each other a glance that only him and I could understand before trying to change the subject. "Pass that shit," I said, trying to calm my nerves.

"His sister Tori said she got a clue on who did it but that she was a lil drunk that night and didn't get the name of the dude she think had something to do with it. But she told the investigators that she would definitely remember his face if she saw him," he went on to say.

He just fucked up my weekend and he aint even know it.

"They better catch them niggas before I do," Tugg said. I wanted to pop that nigga and leave his ass somewhere in Ohio but I had to play my cards right cause this shit was getting real. As we made it back to the city my thoughts were all over the place. I wanted to call the bitch Tori, go kidnap her and knock her off but, I had to get a plan together to kill Tugg before he found out me and JG had something to do with his cousin getting killed. We had to be careful because one slip could have both of us gone. We needed to move fast.

After we got back home and dropped Tugg off, Me and JG had been talking about what we should do every chance we got. He wanted to just go Rambo style but I knew it was a way we could get away with all 3 m's. After hearing what Tugg told me, I sold my car and copped me a '04 black on black SS Monte Carlo. I also quit wearing my chain and tried to stay as low key as possible.

Andrea was noticing the changes in me and was wondering why I was starting to stay in the house so much. I would tell her bullshit like, "I think I'm falling in love," just to get her off my back and it was working. I ain't know she was already deep in love with me and saw me as her man, but I knew I was playing with fire by throwing the love word around. I ain't give a fuck though because I had definitely become a certified trap star in less than a year and minus that bitch Tori being able to point me out in a line-up, I was living good. As the holidays were creeping up Andrea and I had made plans to spend Thanksgiving at my friend's house and Christmas at her people's. The Tuesday before Thanksgiving she asked me to take her to get her hair done by the Africans. I told her to be ready when I came back from running my "errands". By the time I went out and came back home she was ready. We headed to the inner city where I was supposed to be dropping her off at the shop, but as we were pulling up, I saw Susie coming out the variety store next to the hair shop with a baby. I gave Drea $300 for her hair and kissed her goodbye. I couldn't help but notice Susie had gained some weight but she still looked good. She couldn't see me because of the 5% tints I had but I watched her walk right to the purple Sebring I was blocking in. Damn, I thought to myself, could it be? I hadn't seen her in a year but staring at her kind of triggered some old emotions. She stared at my car after securing the baby in the car seat probably wondering if I was gone let her out. I let down my window and said "What's up beautiful?" I could've swore I seen tears form in her eyes as she jumped in her car. I was lost for a second. I aint wanna get out and risk Drea coming out here and causing hell, but my heart wouldn't let me move to let Susie out that parking spot. I had to say something to her so I got out. I walked up to her window and seen a face full of tears, I tried to open the door but it was locked. I told her I wasn't gone move so she may as well talk to me. It was a couple minutes before she let the window down. "What the fuck you want with me Darius?" she said.

"Why you acting like that, what I do to you Susie?"

"You left us you selfish ass nigga," she cried.

"Us, who the fuck is us?" I said not wanting to believe the obvious.

"Me and your son," she said pointing to lil homie in the back seat. I guess the scène caused everybody in the salon to come out because a crowd had formed and Drea was looking crazy with her hair everywhere.

"Who the fuck is that D?" she said. I couldn't even answer her cause apparently, the bitch that was doing her hair was none other than the infamous Tori who was starring a hole through me tryna figure out where she knew me from. “Did you say his name was D?” she repeated while reaching for her cell phone. I grabbed Dread by the arm and forced her in the car. I took one last look at my so-called son, hopped in my Monte' and burnt rubber. Andrea was rambling on and on about why u was still in the parking lot hollering at some “bitch” and how I knew Tori while I was doing 70 in a 35 and my mind doing 100. “Shut the fuck up!" I yelled at her in a tone she never heard from me. Everything went quiet but I knew shit was about to hit the fan.

"Does the bitch who was in the salon with you know where you live?" "Who, and why the fuck..." I cut her off in mid-sentence, "Shut-the-fuck-up and listen to me!" I had her full attention now. "Does the bitch who was pulling out her phone know that you fuck with me or where you live?"

"No, but can you please explain to me what's going on? I've done nothing but been loyal to you from day one," she said.

"You fuck with all these different bitches and think I don't know but I do. I just don't trip cause you don't bring that shit to my doorstep. Nigga, I love you and will never cross you. I would do anything for you but it's time that we get some type of understanding of our relationship Darius. I told you the first night we fucked that I wasn't a little girl who you could just do whatever you wanted to do to! I'm a rider my nigga, if I fuck with you I fuck with you the long way just let me know what's up." I heard the sincerity in her voice, but I wasn't sure about putting my life in her hands like that. It wasn't that I aint trust her, it was that I aint trust nobody. I couldn't show her my whole hand yet but I had a card for her ass. "Look ma, I'm in the middle of a fucked-up situation and I don't really want you to get caught up in it. I'm really feeling you and want you to be wifey but I got some serious trust issue. I got a lot going on in my life that you don't know about."

"Like what, you can tell me anything. You gotta have some type of trust in me to leave your drugs and your safe at my house. I'm not dumb D. I know you got a nice amount of money in there. Don't you think I would've been set you up if I wanted to? I just want to be loved and although you don't show it, I know you have some type of love for me. I'm in love with you baby, haven't you realized that yet? I just want to see you happy. Is there anything I can do to help your situation?" she was playing right to my hand but I still had to be careful.

"How close are you to Tori?"

"She just do my hair, why are you fucking her?, I seen how she was looking at you out there and who was the bitch in the Sebring?" She was grilling me hard! I was ready to go all in with this bitch fuck it! if she was to start tripping she would have to go too!

"We gone talk about this in the house," I told her. I had to buy some time to make sure I was making the right move cause if this plan I had backfired it could get ugly. Fifteen minutes later we were in the crib. "Roll up a blunt and get comfortable," I told her. She returned to the living room with the blunt and a see-through teddy on.

"First let me ask you if you really love me or were you just caught up in the moment earlier in the car," I said.

"Yes, I really love you Darius," she said.

"Okay, do you really wanna be with me regardless of my situation?"

"I been fucking with you this long and I'm ready to be more than I am to you. I feel like I'm woman enough to be everything you need." "Aight, the chick I was hollering at earlier is who I was fucking with before we started kicking it. That was my first time seeing her in over a year, so when I saw her

I was caught off guard. I had to say something to her cause I seen her with that baby."

She passed me the blunt and I hit it a couple times before I started back talking.

"When I hopped out to talk to her she told me that I was the father of her child." I could see the hurt in her eyes but she took it like a G.

"Okay I can deal with that because that was before us, but are you sure it's your baby?" she asked.

"I don't know cause like I said, I aint seen her in over a year and I really ain't have time to ask questions cause of how the scene unfolded."

"Yeah what was up with that? Why you act like that when you saw Tori?"

I had to hit the blunt a couple more times before I said what I said.

"I don't really know Tori, but she kinda got my life in her hands right now."

"What you mean by that?"

"What I'm bout to tell you can't leave this house babe."

"I told you, you can trust me and I would never cross you. I see you as my man and I would do anything for my man."

"Aight that's cool because I do need you."

"To do what?"

"Just listen. Last summer I was in the mix of a homicide and Tori is the only person who can actually put me on the scene. Word on the street is she been looking for me but she never knew my name or anything about me till you screamed out my name today at the shop. She still don't have much on me other than what I drive or that I fuck with you. I need you to set her up for me so I can get at her and clear my name up." I knew I was taking a chance but I felt like this was my best option. "Did you actually commit the homicide?" she asked.

"No but I know enough about the law to know that her saying I did it, is enough to get me a life sentence."

"So you want me to help you murder somebody, just because you scared to go to trial for somebody you didn't murder? This aint making sense to me baby."

I was getting nervous cause this shit wasn't going how I planned on it going. "

It's something you aint telling me baby, you gone have to be 100 with me." She continued to say.

"Okay I was there but I didn't pull the trigger, somebody I was with did but her putting me on the scene is enough to get me fucked up."

"So where's he at?"

"That's irrelevant." I was getting irritated by her questioning and thinking I had made a mistake by telling her this shit.

"How I know you aint using me to get to her?"

"Because I didn't know you knew her till today. This shits a total coincidence," I said.

"How I know you ain't gone cross me and try to kill me after you kill her, then go back to your little bitch in the Sebring?" She was far from dumb but I had to respect the game.

"I guess you gotta trust me baby like I'm trusting you by telling you all this. For all I know you could double cross me by telling Tori or even the cops. I'm a loyal nigga to those who loyal to me, its death before dishonor and I stand on that."

She looked me in the eyes and said, "it's the same here baby."

"So you down for me?" I asked.

"Long as you promise to make me number one and always be there for me?"

"I promise, you gone be the only one baby!" I said as I felt our relationship go to a whole new level. After the blunt went out she immediately pulled my dick out and made it disappear in her mouth. I grabbed a handful of her hair and started to control the back of her head while she positioned herself to where I could use my freehand to play with that pussy. She must've came two or three times before I exploded in her mouth. Like a pro she swallowed every drip and kissed the head as she was coming up for air. She grabbed my hand and led me into the bedroom where we both got completely naked. She got on the edge of the bed and bent over while fingering herself, that quickly got me aroused as I slid all 10 inches of my third leg into her healthy shaved pussy, with my feet planted on the floor and her knees on the bed I admired that phat ass in the air as I tried to reach places she never knew existed. She threw that ass back though and looked back at me like I couldn't handle it. She was biting her bottom lip and bouncing her ass like I was touching her spine. That shit was turning me on more motivating me to be the best she ever had. That thought made me go harder. I slapped her ass a couple times and she started to become very submissive. Before I knew it, her head was damn near against the wall and somehow I had managed to be at the head of the bed where the pillows were at, still pounding her. "Take it out and let me suck it," she said. I had no problem with that, I pulled it out and she turned around and gave me some head that was sure to have me home every night. After she got every drop out of me I was sure I had played my cards the right way. When we were done she got up, got a hot towel and cleaned up our mess then got back in the bed and curled up under me.

"Please don't hurt me," she whispered as we were dozing off. I just laid back thinking of how we were going to put our plan into action and told her, "just trust me."

Chapter 9

The next morning, Andrea was still asleep when I woke up. I sat up in the bed and just stared at her for a while thinking about last night's conversation. Was I tripping or is this the right move to make I asked myself. If she went through with this, it was no going back we would be bonded forever. Going back really wasn't an option now! What would JG think? Should I even tell him or should I wait till we handled Tori. I had a lot on my mind and for the first time in a long time it wasn't money. I was getting so comfortable that I had been slacking on meeting all my people. I got up to check my safe. I hadn't even been counting how much I had. I was just putting bands of 2500's up every chance I got. As the safe opened I was proud of how far I came. I started grabbing the bundles and separating them into stacks of 10,000. I had 85,000 saved up, a half of brick of cocaine and 3 pounds of dro. Life had been good to me, but I had to handle this situation so I can enjoy my shit. I had to go holla at my mom's. It seemed like the deeper I got into the streets the more I got away from my family. I decided to leave 25 Gs, go buy another safe and get an apartment in my sister's name that only me and her knew about. I needed to spend some time with them and spend some time with Drea.

By the time I had closed the safe back up she was getting up. I told her to get herself together so we can bounce. I gave her keys to the Monte and told her to drive me to my storage where the Chevy was. The Chevy had been sprayed burnt orange and had some 24's dubs on it. I didn't want to drive it because so much was going on but right now I had to. As she was dropping me off I peeled her off 3 Gs and told her to "go shopping and handle that!" I headed to the city with $57,000 in cash, in a car that was begging for attention. Luckily, I made it to my moms with no incident. I walked in and everyone was happy to see me. I chilled over there for a minute before I called my little sister into her room. "I need you to put this up for me and don't let anybody know what it is." I gave her 4 bags with 50 Gs in them all together and peeled her off a G for herself. I gave my brother and younger sister $500 apiece and gave moms $2500 before heading out. I called JG, "What up bro?" he answered, sounding excited to hear from me.

"Where you at?" I asked.

"At my sisters, why?"

"Meet me at the club, I'm bout to be there in 5 minutes," I said. "Aight." He saw me and hopped in the passenger side.

"Bout time you pulled this mufucka out," he hollered.

"I don't wanna be in it but I gotta do me right now," I said.

"What the fuck you been doing?"

"I been stacking bro, tryna stay out the way"

"That's what's up, you been seeing that nigga Tugg around?"

"Naw, he locked up for probation violation. He got like 90 days."

"DAMN! WE NEED TO GET AT HIM ASAP! "I told him.

"WHY BRO?

"Nigga you know why, remember ol girl Tori from the club that night?" "Yeah, what about her?"

"She does my girl hair and I ran into her recently. She knows my face and my name and if she holler at Tugg before we do I'm sure they a link the puzzle together."

"Damn bro, we need to find her quick, FUCK HIM."

'I'm 2 steps ahead of you lil bro. I been distant for a reason, that bitch days are numbered, trust me."

"You good? You need me to handle it?"

"Naw I got it but just stay low till I holla back at you."

"Okay bro; be careful," he said as he hopped out.

With that I felt a little better so I headed back to my side of town.

Chapter 10

As I rode down east on 34th street, I couldn't help but to think about Tori as I passed the salon. She was a pretty mufucka that I wouldn't mind fucking but that clearly wasn't going to happen in this lifetime. I had a bullet with her name on it. That sexy bitch had to go! I called Drea to check up on her. "Hello," she answered on the first ring.

"What up baby?"

"On my way to get my nails done."

"Aw you call ol girl yet?" I asked her.

"Yeah she want me to come up to the shop to finish getting my hair done. She asked how I knew you." "What you tell her?" "That I met you at the club last week and that I was just using you to get my hair done and whatever else I can get." "Did she go for it?" I asked. "I don't know, she sounded like she wanted to ask me some more shit about you so I flipped the script on her and asked her how she knew you."

"What she say?"

"She said she think you fucked with some bitch named Kia who's her cousin."

"That lying ass bitch," I said.

"Don't trip baby, we gone get her," she said.

"I know, just be careful and don't act to different around her, she sneaky." "Okay, I'm a call you when I leave."

"Do that," I said before hanging up.

With some time to spare I decided to go by Susie's crib and see what's up with her. Pulling up into her driveway I noticed the Sebring parked on the street. I got out and knocked on the door.

"Who is it?" a male voice screamed from inside the house.

"It's Darius," the door opened and lil Q stood on the other side of it with no shirt on and a nappy ass fro.

"What up lil bro," I said. "What's up D?" as he stepped to the side to let me in. "Your sister here?"

"Yeah, she upstairs, but what up with you, I heard you out east killing the niggas with the work. It must be true because that Chevy looking good out there."

I chuckled a bit as I tried to read the lil nigga. I heard he been running round robbing niggas but I wasn't worried bout that. I was wondering if he knew I had stole the Preacher Man from him.

"I'm maintaining, just tryna make it like the next man," I said.

"You think you can put me on? I got the customers but I aint got no steady work or nobody to get none from," he said.

"Here take my number and call me in a few days, we can make something happen," I told him.

"Aight, sis upstairs with Lil D," he said.

"Lil D?"

"The baby!" he replied.

"Oh." I made my way up the stairs and knocked on her door, it was cracked a little so it opened enough for me to see in.

"What?" she answered not knowing it was me standing in the door way watching her play with the baby.

"What's up with you?" I said in a lower than usual tone, for some reason I felt awkward than a mufucka. She looked up saw me and rolled her eyes hard as hell. I sat on the edge of the bed.

"Why you aint tell me you had a baby?"

"Cause me or my baby don't need you," she said.

"Is that how you gone act? You don't love me no more?"

"Don't come over here with that whack ass game, matter of fact what do you want? Why are you here?"

"I wanna see my son Sue, quit playing."

"Nigga you up and leave me and pop up a year later talking this shit. You could have brought some pampers or something but I'm glad you didn't cause we don't need NOBODY who will just pop up and leave us like that anyway! Gone back out east with that bitch you been staying with."

"Look ma, I aint come to argue or fight with you. I'm sorry shit played out like it did. I never knew you was pregnant and you know I didn't mean to leave you like that. Shit happened fast and changed even faster. I still love you but I aint here to beg for you back. I really aint even here for you, I'm here to accept my responsibilities as a man! True enough I did just up and leave and not even contact you but that was something that just happened. I aint see you going out your way to reach out to me though. I'm sure you could of found me if you really wanted too.

I always told you that you let your pride get in the way of what's important sometimes and you make bad decisions cause of it. You think I don't wanna be in my child's life? I told you how I felt about never meeting my daddy and how I didn't want be shit like him and you do me like this? When was you gone tell me Susie?"

"I was waiting for the right time."

"Miss me with that old ass excuse. It's been a year, when do you think the right time was gone come?"

"Wha, wha, wha..." we had the baby crying with our arguing. I watched as she carefully picked him up and cradled him till he stopped crying. "Can I hold him?" She sat him in my arms and I got a different type of feeling as I looked into his eyes and seen my reflection. For the first time ever I felt like I had my own little family but I knew it wasn't right because the girl that I really loved was running round town conspiring a potential homicide for me. I had 99 problems and 3 of them were definitely bitches.

"What's his name?" I asked her.

"Darius Lamont Miles Jr." I gave him back to her and told her I had to make a few runs.

"So, are you going to be a part of our life or is this how it's gone be?" she said with an attitude.

"Let me handle this shit I got going on and I promise we gone get everything straightened out. I want him to have the best of everything and I'm a do all I can to see that that happens." I said really meaning it.

"All he need is for you to be here with him."

I was silenced cause I always said I would be there for my child whenever I had one, but I didn't expect it to be like this.

"I'm a be there but I gotta take care of some shit first and after that I'm a get you outta here and in your own spot."

"And where you gone be? With that other bitch?"

"Chill out, just let me do me, I got us!"

"You been doing you anyway, so that aint nothing new."

"I can't win with you, can I?" I said.

"What are you trying to win? This aint no fucking game nigg!."

I reached in my pocket gave her a couple Gs and told her to grab whatever she needed for her and the baby. I told call me if she needed me then kissed her on the cheeks and left out her room. She woulda went on forever if I aint just leave and I aint have time for that.

On the way out, Q told me he would holla at me and I said cool. I didn't really trust him and I needed to get away from her. I got in the car, stopped by the nearest gas station, grabbed a black and mild and drove out east, my nerves was shot.

CHAPTER 11

Andrea

As I left out the Asians spot from getting my nails done I was feeling good about life and myself. I had a boss and I was #1 in his life. After all I have been through I deserved this type of life. I was gone do whatever I had to do to keep my position, if that meant getting Tori set up then that's what it was gone be. She was cool but she wasn't fucking me or taking care of me. Darius was my ticket to lavish living and I wasn't tryna loose that. On my way to finish getting my hair done I started thinking about my cousin Krissy. I hadn't talked to her since me and D been getting serious and I was missing her. Since he peeled me off a couple Gs I thought it would be nice to go pick her up.

"What up cuz?"

" Hey cousin!"

"What up Kris, what you been up too.

"Shit, just got a job at Burger King and enrolled to start Ivy Tech next semester for business class. What you been up to? You aint been calling me since you got a man."

"I know I'm sorry but I wanna make it up to you today. I'm coming to get you in a couple hours where you gone be?"

"Who car you driving?" Krissy said, "I know he aint bought you no car?" "Girl I got access granted, he gave me the keys to his shit and some money to go shopping. You wanna go or not?"

"Hell yea if you gone buy me something."

"Bitch where you at?"

"I'll be at my mamas in a hour."

"Okay," I hung up the phone and went into the shop. It seemed like all eyes were on me as I put on a phony smile and walked up to Tori. She had a white girl in her chair who looked like she would die to be black. "Hey girl, your next, it will be about ten minutes," she said. I took a seat and listened to the hoes gossip about everything that was going on this side of town.

I was glad to finally be in the chair after hearing the bitches hate on everybody and they mami.

"You still want the kinky twist?" she asked me.

"No, I want you to start my dreads."

"You sure"

"Yeah"

"Okay, it's your hair, that nigga must have ya mind fucked up."

"What nigga?"

"Don't play stupid Andrea, that fine ass nigga who car you driving." "Oh, my sponsor?"

"Looked like more than that the way he grabbed your arm, he was acting like yo daddy." This bitch was pissing me off but I had to keep my cool.

"He can be my daddy long as he taking care of me, but I seen you looking at him like you wanted some of that dick."

"Maybe if he wasn't yours already I'd give him some of this pussy, he is sexy."

"I'm down to share him if you down to share that." We had got lost in our own private conversation and by the look on her face she was getting a lil nervous.

"Un-Un, I don't get down like that," she said in a low voice.

"Like what?" I said.

"That girl on girl."

"We aint got to touch each other, trust me when I say he got enough dick for both of us."

"You crazy girl."

"Don't knock it till you try it, you might love it," I said. She changed the subject but I knew she was interested. We continued with small talk till she was done. A couple hours had passed before she was done.

"Thanks Tori, I like this look," I said as I looked in the mirror.

"You a have to get them done at least twice a month to make sure they lock up the right way."

"What I owe you"

"Just give me 50 I usually charge 80 to start dreads but I fucks with you."

"There you go." I handed her a 100-dollar bill and told her, "I fucks with you too". I mouth the words 'call me' and blew her a kiss as I walked away from the booth. Surprisingly she whispered, 'I will' and winked at me. I knew I had her where I wanted her.

Tori

I couldn't believe this diking ass bitch just tried to come on to me. I always knew it was something funny about her ass. I think her and that bitch she call her cousin be fucking on the low. I don't give a fuck though, because she gone lead me right to them niggas who killed my baby daddy. Ol gold-digging bitch don't even know what the fuck she got herself into. I guess I'm a have to take matters in my own hands because the police damn sure aint gone bring no justice to me and my daughter. I had to make a visit to the only person who I knew could help me. Knowing we was gone be open all night cause of thanksgiving I went to the Marion County Jail on my break.

TUGG

"Shawn Tugglamore, visit!" yelled the C.O. Who the fuck was coming to see me, I aint even really fuck with my BM like that, plus I was about to get out in a couple days. Fuck it, it beat sitting in this block all day. I went to the computer screen.

"What up T," I said as I picked up the phone.

"Hey Tugg, how you doing?"

"I'm good, what bring you down here? the investigators still calling you and shit?"

"No, they probably gave up on it, you know they don't care about black on black crime."

"Yeah, what up though?" Is it safe to talk on these phones?" Tori asked. "Yeah, they aint recording. Why, what up?"

"You know that night Jamal got shot I saw who did it."

She had my full attention now. "Yeah I heard you was out there."

"Well, I kinda know who it is and how to get him but I can't do it by myself and I don't trust nobody else. When you get out?"

"This weekend." I told her.

"Okay, do you want me to try to find them?" How many of them is it? Who are they?" I started asking.

"Well I don't know the actual shooter name or where he at, but the dude that was with him name is D. I do his girl hair, they from out east." "Is he skinny and got a fade?"

"Yeah, he drives a Monte Carlo."

"A Monte Carlo?"

"Yeah, it's a new boy."

"Did you see the shooter?"

"Yeah they were all up on me at the club that night. He was lighter than D and had gold and braids."

"JG," I said out lout but more to myself. I had been hearing it was them niggas but I aint want to believe it.

"Aight, stay away from them niggas and keep ya ears to the street. I be out in a couple days, I'll call you when I touchdown."

"Okay."

She got up and left. I slammed the phone on the receiver ferociously and stormed back to the dorm, I felt betrayed and crossed! These niggas knew they killed my cousin when we was riding to Cincinnati. They coulda easily killed my ass and left me in the Ohio River. I wondered why they didn't but I was glad they didn't. They fucked up. I went back to the block and locked myself in the cell where I would stay till I got out. I made a promise to myself and to lil cuz that I would kill both of these niggas for him! I PUT THAT ON MY LIFE!

Chapter 12

Andrea

When I left the shop, I went to pick up Krissy. We went to Castleton Square Mall and a had a mini shopping spree. I bought her a few Pink outfits and a couple pairs of shoes and I bought myself some Derion outfits and some heels. It felt good to be with my cousin but she was my best friend too. We use to talk about everything but I couldn't tell her what was going on in my life. She told me how everything was going for her and I was happy for her. Even though we were going in two different directions, we were both happy in our own way.

When we got to the parking lot my phone rang, After fumbling through my Coach purse, I answered it. It was Darius.

"What up baby?"

"Hey boo."

"Where you at?"

"Leaving the mall up north with Krissy."

"Aw tell her I said what up."

"She said 'Hi'"

"When you heading back to the crib?" he asked.

"I should be there in about half-hour. I'm done doing everything I had to do."

"Everything?"

"Yeah but um!!!"

"I get it we'll talk later," he said.

"Okay love you."

"Love you too!"

"Damn, yall sound like a happy couple." Krissy said after I hung up. "Yeah, we building something special, I hope he the one."

"Don't settle for less if he aint."

"You already know cuz, you already know."

I turned up the Keisha Cole and dropped her off before heading back home. I was wondering...would he be the one.

Chapter 13

Darius

As I sat in the crib watching sports center, I heard Drea coming in the house. I was shocked at how good she was looking with her new hair style, "Damn baby I Like that look, maybe I'll start mines."

"Well Tori sure aint gone be the one starting them for you."

"You saying that like she already "dead!"

"Naw but I'm gone get her."

"When cause I'm ready to take matters in my own hands baby. This shit stressing me out. The faster we get this over with the faster we over on with our lives. You think she still at the shop?"

"I don't know want you to be too obvious and blow the whole plan. I know she got a clue of what's going on"

"I told her I got both ways and that I was more than willing to share you with her so she..." you told her what?" I immediately got shitty, "Why the fuck would you tell her some shit like that, she gone see right through that bullshit. She been doing yo hair all this time, how all a sudden, the nigga that's a suspect to her people's murder is fucking one of her clients? She see me dropping you off and the next day you tryna get her to have a threesome with us? What the fuck was you thinking Drea?"

"I was tryna be down for you and do what you asked me to do."

"I told you don't start acting different around her and you did just that."

"Well how else was I supposed to get close to her? It aint like we friends she just do my hair."

"Okay, okay, just chill out we gone figure it out, you aint tell yo cousin shit did you?"

"No, I aint like that, I know how serious this is that's why I just want it to get over with."

As I stood in the room listening to her I started second guessing myself and felt my stress level rose.

"Aight baby stay in the crib till I come back, don't talk to nobody bout none of what's going on and don't talk to Tori either. If she calls you ignore her. "Okay." I kissed her on the cheek and was out the door. Soon as I got in my car I called JG to let him know I was coming to pick him up, this sit was getting deeper and deeper by the day. Something had to shake soon! On my way to pick up JG, I took my normal route to the city. Riding pass the salon I noticed it was still open. That was odd as fuck to me, but I guess bitches was trying to get they shit done for Thanksgiving weekend, which was understandable cause it was gone be helly parties going down, but that was the last thing on my mind...

I pulled up on JG who was at his usual hang out spot and we just rode out. I stopped at the Amoco to grab some blunts and get some gas. When I got back in the car, he started rolling the weed up. I turned the music down and had to tell him what I didn't want to tell him.

"Bro, I think I fucked up."

"What you do?"

"Man, some crazy ass shit." Seeing the look on my face he studied my expression to see if I was bullshitting or not.

"Nigga, what you do?" Man, I tried to get Andrea to set up Tori but this dumb ass bitch may have blown our cover."

"What the fuck would you do that for?" he paused and starred at me, "when I already asked, did you need me to care of her? She aint blow our cover, you did nigga! I told you bout pillow talking with these bitches bro! Is the pussy that good that you willing to put yo life on the line for it? If that bitch get us ran up, it's on you nigga!"

"Chill out that shit, she don't know you had shit to do with it and the bitch Tori aint got a clue of where you at or shit else about you," I said. "Nigga you the one who told me her and Tugg gone link everything together, how you know she aint already hollered at that nigga?" "Cause my bitch just got her hair done today and that bitch still at the salon."

"How you know that?"

"Cause I rode by there on the way to pick you up and that mufucka was still open; you know these hoes tryna get they shit nailed for the holiday."

"Nigga we staking that mufucka out and getting that bitch tonight soon as she leaves!"

"We can't do that in this car."

"I know, pullup to the Walmart," he told me. When we got to Walmart, he told me to park. We went in and bought two pairs of gloves, skullies and hoodies. On the way out he handed me the bag and said, "Keep yo eyes open and watch for the police." I got in the car and just watched him walk around the parking lot looking lost, after a few minutes he came and got in the car. "I'm bout to snatch this car just follow me." He grabbed a skully and a hoodie and put them on and put the gloves in his pocket. 'Watch out for the rotating camera on the top of the building," I told him. He put the hood on his head and got out. It took him no time to get the little Neon started. When I saw him peel out the parking lot I eased my way into traffic behind him. He called me as we rode back-to-back to our side of town.

"Hello"

"Where you gone park ya car at?" We headed toward mama's backyard and I parked and was ready to get in with him. He let the window down as I approached the passenger side and told me to grab the bag out my car and opened the door for me.

"Nigga quit playing crazy and put the fucking gloves and shit on bro!" He sounded annoyed and I was nervous as hell but I knew what had to be done and it was no turning back.

"I got a couple guns stashed in my bitch crib in the apartments, we gone grab them and go wait on the bitch to come out, aight?"

"Whatever bro."

As we pulled up to the apartments and he went in the corner apartment, I couldn't help but think of what we had already done and what we was about to do. I was all in, fuck it!

JG

I couldn't believe this nigga told his bitch he was involved in a homicide. We just met these hoes last summer. That's my brother and I'll do anything for him but he don't think sometimes and he can't hold water. All it takes is for his lil girlfriend to slip-up and tell one person then he's done. I don't believe he would take me down with him but I can't see him going down like that. That's why Tori gotta go ASAP and I'm a make sure she get got! I could tell he was a lil nervous when I stole the car and told him the plan, but he will be aight!

<u>Darius</u>

When JG got back to the car and showed me the artillery, I thought we was gone be taking out a whole block.

"Damn nigga what we need all that for."

"Aint no telling who gone be coming outta there bro, our life on the line, it's us or them my nigga."

"Let's go then, I'm ready to get this shit over with." We pulled into the salon shop, they was still packed to be so late. There was traffic coming in and out of the shop and the candy store next to it so we just pulled in and parked backward where we really couldn't be seen though the tints but had a clear view of the shops front door. As we sat waiting we smoked blunt after blunt and cigarette after cigarette with the radio on real low. There wasn't much talking but I could tell he had shit on his mind. As it got darker outside I got more anxious and nervous. The parking lot was getting emptier and it was only 3 cars out including ours. When we saw the lights in the shop go out, Tori and another lady came out and turned around to lock the doors, JG said, "Is that her?" "Yea I think so."

"You get the other bitch and I'ma get her. Make sure you kill her."

We checked our weapons and got out just as they were turning around, "Tori!" I yelled.

before she could respond JG let off round after round into her torso, "bop" "bop"

"bop" as the witness start screaming I lifted my arm to squeeze the trigger but I couldn't.

"Boc" "Boc" 'Boc" "Boc"

I heard the rounds and saw JG aiming the 40 right at her.

"Here" he passed me his strap.

"Finish her off" and let's go."

I aimed at her and squeezed twice before hopping back into the neon. I immediately lit up a square as he drove patiently back towards the apartments.

"Nigga, why you freeze up," he screamed at me.

"I don't know bro I just did."

"Don't worry about it bro you a get over it, but don't tell nobody and I mean nobody about this bro! OKAY?" he said looking dead in my eyes. "I aint. Just drop me off to my car."

Chapter 14

When I got back to my car I took off the hoody, gloves and skully and left them with JG. He told me he would get rid of the car, the guns and the clothes and for me to go on about my life as normal. Riding back out east all I could think about was 2 ladies who wasn't even 30 yet gunned down for nothing, basically.

I thought about my two little sisters and the what-ifs but I quickly lost these thoughts when the "what-if it was Tori setting me up or snitching on me" crossed my mind. I turned up my radio and rapped along out loud with Lil Boosie.

"Hope I make it before y'all take it, my pistol off safety, yall niggas gone me get to spraying…" I was caught up and knee deep in a fucked-up situation.

When I got home, Drea was up sitting in the living room watching the news. Soon as I walked through the door she jumped up and hugged me with tears in her eyes. Nothing had to be said. I could tell she knew something had happened and when she opened her mouth to start speaking I just put my finger over her mouth and said, "Don't worry about it, everything gone be all right."

Chapter 15

Thanksgiving '06

Thanksgiving Day seemed gloomy to me this year. It was rainy and cloudy outside and the apartments were quieter than usual. The news had been calling last night events "Thanksgiving Ambush" and wouldn't stop broadcasting it. I felt bad, but in my head it seemed like the right thing to do. We got dressed and headed to my mother's house for dinner.

When we got there, I was happy to see my family together, especially my sisters. Seeing the smiles on everyone's face and feeling the holiday spirit brightened up my day. JG was there and me, him and my little brother KD played Halo with my nephew. My sister's, Mother and Drea were playing scramble. Everyone laughed and joked for hours waiting on my mother's husband to finish the food. Finally, it was time to eat and we all gathered around the table holding hands as my mother lead us in prayer. She was going on and on about everything she was thankful for and how she was very grateful that it wasn't her daughters that were killed last night and that all her kids were together. It was ironic that those girls being killed was possibly the reason we were altogether. It was crazy how life worked but I was a firm believer in the saying that everything happened for a reason and that was keeping me happy and for the moment. After we ate everybody was sitting around, back to joking. I called little sis into the back room and told her I would come and pick her up Monday from school to go take care of some business for me. After everybody said their goodbyes JG, Myself and Drea headed outside.

"What yall bout to get into?" JG asked.

"We finna go spend some time with my family," Drea answered before I could respond.

"Yea, she got me for the day bro, you wanna come? Krissy might be there," I said in a jokingly manner. He smirked before saying, "Nah yall enjoy yall day together, but let me holla at you for a minute bro. See you later sis and tell Krissy to call me."

"Okay bro, be careful, and yall hurry up I ain't bout to be waiting in the car all day," she said before walking to the Chevy.

"What up bro, you cool?" he asked me.

"I guess, it aint like I got a choice not to be," I said.

"Shake it off man. Bitches get killed every day in the hood. You'll get over it. It was you or her, remember that."

"Yeah you right. What you bout to get into though?"

"Shit,Just go check my traps and chill with my crew."

"Alright I'll call you later lil bro, be careful."

"Okay, make sure you do that and keep ya mouth shut."

"Lil nigga you act like you the big brother," I said smiling.

"I know," he said arrogantly showing all his gold fronts before walking off. The bond we had was like no other, it was like an opposite attract type of thing, but that was us and we was down for each other right or wrong!

Chapter 16

TUGG

"Double Homicide on the East side" was all I heard as I laid on my bunk stressed out about missing my sons first Thanksgiving. I hopped up and went in the dayroom to see the breaking news.

"Late last night 21-year-old Tori Webster and 26-year-old Lauren Taylor's bodies were ambushed and gunned down in front of the mini plaza on the Eastside of Indy. At the time, there are no suspects. IMPD and the families are offering $10,000 rewards for any information that will lead to arrest in cases. Whoever did this showed no regards for human life as both victims were shot multiple times in the face and upper torso. There were three different types of casings found at the scene but detectives are unsure of how many suspects there are. The community is urging anyone with information to come forward."

I couldn't believe it. These niggas was out there going crazy. Never in a million years would I have thought they would turn into straight- killers.

I was dumbfounded.

I couldn't figure out for nothing in the world why they didn't kill me, but I realized that although I was locked-up, I was blessed to be alive. This bitch had just come to see me yesterday. This shit was fucking my head up. I know they were looking for me now. I had to come up with a hell of a plan before they let me out of here because it as a warzone out there and I don't know if I was ready for it. I aint have no choice thought, these niggas done killed my lil cuz and his baby mama. That nigga D been getting the big head ever since he moved out east. Got a lil money and got beside his-self. I gotta trick for his ass though! And JG in the hood every day acting like he can't be touched. I'm a kill two birds with one stone.

DARIUS:

We got to Drea's people house around 6:00 PM and were gone by 8:00. I was surprised by how down to earth her moms was. You could tell they were straight out the hood and I liked that. Drea was happy that I bonded with her family so well and that we had such a good time today. Im not ready to go home yet," she said.

"What you wanna do?" I asked.

"Let's go to the movies."

"Let's go it's your day!" We went to the movies and went to get a hotel room afterwards just to get away. We drank Remy and smoked all night before relaxing in the hot tub. We talked about everything from our past to our dreams and just enjoyed the moment.

After we got out the tub she treated me to a private show and sexed me like I had just come home from doing a 5 year bid. We got done and she laid on my chest and asked me how long I planned on living the way I was living?

"You got a problem with all this?" I answered jokingly referring to the 5-Star room we were in that overlooked the city. She gave me the serious look and said "Boy you know what I'm talking about. Don't get me wrong, this shit is nice but when you in a position like you in, you gotta take advantage of it because it don't last forever."

"I'm taking advantage! I enjoy life every day and now that that problem is out the way I'm ready to go to the next level."

"Then what?"

"What you mean then what? Then we won't have no problems?"

"Why not? Cause you got money? Money ain't everything baby."

"But it makes life easier."

"I understand that but a lot comes with money"

"Yeah like shopping sprees for you and ya cousin, hair-dos, jewelry..." "Cases, haters, stress, murders, you can't just look at the good part of it. I'm telling you this cause I love you and want us to make it to that next level you talking bout, the right way. My brother was a big d-boy and was young like you. He bought me everything I wanted and taught me a lot. You probably think I'm trying to change you or just bitching, but you got a rider and I aint gone fall off cause I aint gone let you fall off. The shit you do for me it's cool and I appreciate it but I been around the block a few times and I grew up around this shit my whole life. My daddy built an empire from scratch with heroin before he was sentenced to life in federal prison in the late nineties. My brother took over and was killed because of his arrogance. I could have easily taken over but I'm not foolish enough to think that I would have any better luck than they did, so I choose to go a different route. I know my mama and lil sister needed me. We went from having it all to Section 8 living. They took everything from us because my father didn't clean any of his money up and my mama was too comfortable to help. I see us in them but I want different result."

"What you saying?"

She sat up and said, "We should make some business plans to invest in different businesses and I'll get a job and go back to school. We can do some legal shit."

"Where you been all my life girl? You may be the key to success."

"You know behind every king is the real shot caller aka the queen."

I aint gone lie, she had me open now cause all I could see was money signs. We called room service to bring a bottle of champagne and a pen and some paper. We toasted to better lives and stayed up for hours writing down business ideas and plans for our future. That night I realized I had a boss bitch that loved me for me and wanted to see me successful, how could I fail?

Chapter 17

JG

Thanksgiving weekend was doing numbers for my trap. I had my own lil crew running my spots and all I had to do was collect the cash. As long as these niggas had my money on time we aint have no problems. I wasn't a flashy nigga, and I aint take no shit, so many of my workers stayed in order because I was loyal to my team. I aint have too many problems and when I did, I handled em out the gate!

I was a lil worried about bro but I knew he would be okay, it aint like thats the first dead body or killer he been around. I was more worried bout the nigga Tugg. We don't know if that bitch Tori hollered at him before we got her or not but we aint have no room for error. For all I know he could be in jail telling everything, so I had a $10,000 tag on his head that only a few mufuckas knew about. I know D thinking about some money or pussy instead of his freedom and that's just him. My freedom meant everything to me, so I stay on top of shit like that and that's what makes us an elite team. I know we aint untouchable but we definitely some young niggas on the rise and I aint tryna let shit stop my come up!

<u>SUSIE</u>

"You have a collect call from…'ITS ME', to accept press 1 to stop these calls press 5…"

"Thank you for accepting this call"

"Hello?"

"What up B.M."

"Hi"

"What you sound so down for? You supposed to be happy to talk to your baby daddy."

"Maybe I would be happy if my baby daddy was out her with me helping me raise our child instead of being in jail for violating his probation because he wanna get high."

"Why you got to go there."

"Because you do dumb shit and make dumb choices and ask dumb ass questions, that irks me!"

"Oh I wasn't a dumb mufucka when you was fucking me, was I? I wasn't a dumb mufucka when you wanted to get high and needed someone to talk to cause you was fucked up over that nigga was I?" "What do you want? Did you call me to talk shit?"

"I'm sorry, we got started on the wrong foot today babe, how are you?" "I'm fine Shawn, now what's up, I know you want something cause that's the only time you call."

"I got a plan for us to make some money."

"I'm listening."

"Okay, you still talk to that nigga?"

" What nigga?"

"Darius"

"Why? You sound like you on some bullshit."

"Naw I'm just tryna get in touch with him."

"Don't call me from jail asking about no other nigga, call me when you out! (CLICK_UP)."

I don't know what the fuck he on. He is so jealous of Darius, he hated him. I regret fucking with his broke –lame ass. When Darius quit coming around the hood I was so mad at him that I started talking to Shawn to piss off D but my plan backfired. This nigga would sit around all night telling me how Darius was fucking all these different bitches and how I never meant anything to him, but all along he was just using me to try to get at D. I can't even muster the strength to tell D that my baby don't belong to him. It's his friends who really hate him because he wants to be him. Now I'm stuck with this clown ass nigga, but D don't know and I'm a use his ass as long as possible. A bitch gotta eat too right? I still love Darius but I feel like he just up and left and said fuck everything we had. I'm supposed to be the bitch on his side instead of that bitch Drea I keep hearing about and everybody knows it. The bitch stole my come up and now I'm stuck in the hood looking like a whore because I was fucking both of them. I know it's only a matter of time before he finds out but it my word against theirs and only two people know the truth.

Tugg

"Tugglamore step into the Corridor."

Why the fuck was the C.O.'s calling me to the hall when my 90 days weren't up until tomorrow? Maybe they had plans on letting me out early or something. I aint know but I got up and went out to see what they wanted. I was escorted to the attorney visiting room. I immediately start to think all types of shit when I saw the two detectives on the other side of the glass. I said a quick prayer that they wasn't gone try to bring up no old shit the day before I got out then picked up the phone.

"What up" I asked.

"Are you Shawn Tugglamore?"

"Yes, why?" "We are the homicide detectives and we have reason to believe that you know about a homicide we have been investigating since the summer."

"What homicide are yall talking about?"

"The murder of Jamal Tugglamore who we believe may be related to you."

"Is that how I'm linked to this, because I have the same last name?" "No, we were informed that last week you had a visit with a Tori Webster, who is now deceased. The recording that you told her was "safe to talk on" is enough evidence to charge you with conspiracy." "Conspiracy? Conspiracy for what? I been in here for the last 3 months. I aint did shit."

"We have reason to believe that you had Tori killed."

"Why would I do that? That's my cousin baby mama."

"We think you had her killed because word on the street is she set Jamal up."

"What?"

"It's something you're not telling us. Help us help you or it will be a long winter."

"I don't know nothing, what can I tell yall?"

"Who is D?"

"D who?"

"D with the "New boy Monte Carlo" from out east who hangs with the lighter guy with golds and braids!" They was serious and they caught me completely off guard. The look on my face told it all. I was in a tight spot but it may help me out.

"Look detectives, I think I can help yall out but what's in it for me?" "You can clear your name from our suspect list and be released tomorrow as planned."

"Okay, what about that reward money they was talking about on the news?"

"You would get the reward money once the conviction is made."

"Okay, from what I know, Tori was at the club talking to D, whose real name is Darius Logan. He was there with JG whom he calls his brother but I don't know if they are really related or know his real name. I guess from all the stories I heard, Jamal didn't like D talking to his baby mama and confronted him in the parking lot then JG came up and shot him. "Do you know anyone else that was there to witness this?" "No." Iis there anything else you want to tell us, like who killed Tori?"

"Like I said I been locked up sir, I definitely wouldn't want her dead but I'm like 90% sure that D and JG had something to do with it, if they didn't do it."

"Okay Mr. Tugglamore, were going to have the officers leave our card in your property in-case you want to get in contact with us. We will keep our eyes on you until we get some type of confirmation of what you told us."

"This is a confidential conversation isn't it?"

"Certainly. we wouldn't want you to come up missing or dead."

"No I aint worried about that, I just don't wanna be known as a snitch." "We understand."

"Okay."

"We'll be in touch about that reward money."

"Cool."

I can't believe I just broke the G-code, was all I was thinking on my way back to the block. They threatened to charge me with conspiracy for knowing who killed my cousin. I don't even know if that's legal but fuck that, I had to do what I had to do cause I wasn't trying to miss my outdate for shit. Plus I could use a couple thousand.

Chapter 18

DARIUS

I can't front, Drea had me wide open and looking at life from a different angle. I could see myself rich in the next five years fucking with her. I was on my way to pick up my sister from school so I could get me another stash spot. All I could think about was taking shit to the next level.

I picked up lil sis and we went to my mamas to get the money then headed up north to the more suburban areas to look for apartments. We rode around for hours before finding some apartment complexes that were nice and had "Move in Today" specials. We went into the office so we could fill out the application and was surprised to be accepted within the next hour. They asked her when she would be ready to move in. She told them ASAP, and all they wanted was a down deposit and next month's rent. We paid up for 6 months and explained that she would be graduating soon and left with the keys and no problem. We headed straight to the

Menards' hardware store to grab a steel safe, then went to the spot.

"Lil sis, me and you are the only people who know about this spot and know the combination to this safe. Its 50 thousand in this bag, I'm putting 20 in here, giving you 2500 and keeping the rest, under no circumstances do you tell anyone about this spot or what goes on in here. I'm a never keep drugs in here cause I don't want you to get caught up in my life like that. This just my stash house and you the only person I trust to know about it, so take that money and go buy yourself some nice things."

"Thanks bro, but I'm tryna get me a lil car so I won't have to be so dependent on no one."

"Do what you wanna do, I got ya back and you know the combination to the safe but try to use it for emergencies only."

After promising to take her car shopping this week, I dropped her off at mama's crib and called JG. "Hello."

"What up lil bro, where you at?", I said.

"I'm at the trap, come thru."

"Aight, I be there in a few." I hated going in any bodies else spot but I had too sometimes. I got there in no time and was let in by his doorman. "What up?"

"Shit tryna get it nephew, what bring you round here, you like a celebrity to these niggas out here."

"Aw man cut it out, I gotta check on lil bro every so often," I said.

"They in there getting high playing the game."

"Aight." I walked to the front of the apartment and all you heard was loud music, niggas talking shit and a couple of bitches talking bout nothing. This wasn't my type of environment because although I wasn't really a killer, a house full people mean a house full of potential witness to me. I called JG to come holla at me in the back, "What you got all these mufuckas around here for."

"Nigga, let me run my shit how I run it, do I tell you how to run yo spots or yo trap?"

"You right my bad, what up though?"

"I'm straight just tryna get it. I thought you was too good for the projects, what you doing down here?"

"I been thinking it's time for us to make a power move."

"I been waiting to hear that, between these two spots I got out here u can't keep enough dope for these junkies. What you got in mind?"

"I think we need to go holla at Peewee, try to get at least a brick or two and go hard for about two or three months without spending shit and see where we at then."

"Who got you thinking like this, Drea?"

I had to laugh a lil cause this nigga knew me like the back of his hand, "Yeah, nigga, that pillow talking paying off. I think I got me one bro, this bitch pops was the man and schooled baby girl on the game. She might get a nigga where he tryna get," I said.

"Aight I'm down but be careful bro. Everybody know bitches almost always got ulterior motives and end up being a niggas downfall."

"Or come-up. Now how much you got to put on the score?"

"You know I run my shit like operations so I break bread with everybody." He said

"Nigga how-much-do-yall-got-right-now?"

"Let me go see what they got on em and run across the lot to holla at my lieutenant lil Earl to see what they got."

"Lil earl from out south?"

"Yeah he hold shit down when I aint around."

"Aight man hurry up, I aint tryna be in here too long."

He left and I went to the living room where the "party" was. I smoked a blunt and flirted with the sexy ladies while the lil niggas played the game. The higher I got the more nervous I got cause the door never stopped the whole time I was there. He had a nice set-up but I didn't feel comfortable. 20 minutes later he came back and we went back to the room.

"I got $17,500 big bro."

"Aight, call Peewee and tell them we coming to holla at them." We made it to Peewee's spot in less than ten minutes.

"What up D, I been asking bout you and wonder when you was gone holla at me."

"I had some shit I had to take care of, I'm here though and I'm ready to eat."

"Talk to me, I'm listening."

"What you gone charge us for 2 whole ones?"

"I'm charging niggas 26.5, flat"

"25, that's the best you can do?" JG said.

"Look since you my main man lil brother I'm a let you get em for 24.5 that's it."

"That's a good number" I said,

"but all we got is about 35 on us right now."

"You got the money right now?"

"Yeah"

"Aight, I'm already cutting yall a deal so I aint gone do no consignment, business is business so don't take it personal but I'm a give yall what yall paying for which is about 1 and a quarter."

"How much will one and a half be?"

"36,750"

"aight, We got that."

"I don't see it."

I went to the car to get my money out my compartment and we counted out 36,750.

Peewee went to the back and came out with a footlocker bag and sat it on the table. We inspected the work then headed back to JGs spot.

We got back to the spot and went straight to the back, "That was a nice score lil bro, I told you I liked that lil nigga Peewee."

"Yeah its time to bubble off this, how we gone split it up though, you in for more than me."

"We use a team lil bro, yo team is my team but we the boss, without you having the play for so low. I wouldnt be able to score like this so we gone cook all this shit up, split it in half and just throw me a couple Gs back after the flip."

"That's love bro."

"Well let's get to work."

"Come in here."

We went in the front room and he cut off the TV and hollered for the doorman to close shop for a while and to send anyone who came by to the other spot. "Let me introduce you to the team, I know it looks like we bullshitting around but these five mufuckas in here are my most trusted workers. These aint just two sexy bitches, they are what we call the brains and the beauty aka our chemist, they do it all from luring niggas in to get wiped-down, put the spots in the names, keep track of every crumb that's sold out this mufucka and most importantly they the ones who gone turn this brick and a half into 3 bricks of B- or C+ crack for us.

They immediately grabbed the bags and headed to the kitchen. "These two youngsters ain't just no average lil niggas. When beauty and the brains get niggas in them rooms, these the nigga who coming in and leaving no witness. Anybody get outta-line, these the niggas who they got to answer to. They learned from me, so you know they ain't gone hesitate to pop that thang. They're brothers, Keith and Kevin and you know unc, the doorman – he's doing all the hand to hand transactions and the little shit like making sure them bitches ain't in there stealing no work."

I was totally impressed; this nigga had a mini factory in the projects. We went back to the back while the bitches got the work ready.

"So whats going on at the spot where lil Carl at?" I asked.

"We keep a lil work over there but that's mostly a weed spot and pill spot, they go crazy for that X out here."

"How many workers he got?"

"Just him and two homies"

"So you got eight workers on yo payroll bro? How you keep food on everybody plater and still have some for yourself at the end of the day?"

"On the average week we profit $7,500, that's 30 Gs in a month off the drugs. I take 10K of that off top, I pay my workers $2500 a month, give my LT $6,000 a month and his workers get $2,000 a month. On top of all that, we usually get two or three licks per month that brings us an extra 20, 30 or sometimes 50 Gs if we do our homework long enough. We just split that up between the whole team evenly, everybody happy at the end of the day. Sometimes it gets rough cause shit don't work out but I'm loyal to them and they loyal to me, so they believe me when I say shit gone get better. I'm sure with this score right here though we aint gone never look back."

"I see you nigga, get ya grind on, whatever work for you. Make sure you tell em 90 days straight is the mission."

"I got em!"

After a couple hours of small talk, the ladies were finally done. Unc called us into the kitchen and what I saw put a smile on my face. It was the most dope I had ever seen, sitting there starting at me.

I looked at these two bitches and would have never thought they were capable of this shit. They had scales out and everything bagged up in ounces. "What it come out to be?" I asked.

"94 ounces of straight drop." I fell in love with these bitches after they said that.

"What are yalls names? I think I love yall!" I said playfully.

"I'm Kia and this Jazzmine."

"I see why they call yall the beauty and the brains, yall gone get us rich." Everybody was laughing and feeling good about our soon to be future. Kia and Jazz was sexy but they were dangerous. I had to stay away from them because I could see myself mixing business with pleasure as long as they were around.

Chapter 19

As the week went by me and Drea had been doing everything together. We mostly stayed in the house and got our hustle on. If I had to make a run and someone called while I was out, I would send em to the house and she would serve me. She had enrolled I an business administration class, besides the four classes she had through-out the week she took classes at home during the night and the shit was coming together. Money was coming in so fast, it was scary. JG and I were consistent with scores and Peewee was consistent with the dope. I was filling up the safe at Drea's crib and at my spot she aint know about.

About a month into my 90 day run, I was dropping my sister off at my mama's crib and shocked to see polices cruises in her driveway. I began to panic immediately. We jumped out the car and ran up the yard to see what was going. "Mama what's up," I asked in a worried tone.

"Are you Darius Logan?" asked one of the officers.

"Yeah why?"

"We have a warrant for your arrest"

"A what? " I said.

"A warrant. Please put your hands on your head and turn around." "Yall got me fucked up, this gotta be a mistake!"

"You're wanted for the murders of Tori Webster and Lauren Taylor and you're wanted for question on another murder that may be linked to those murders."

I could have thrown up, they read me my Miranda Rights, but I was in a daze. My whole life flashed before my eyes, I couldn't get locked up right now, life was too sweet for me. The look in my mama and sister's face almost broke me, but I knew I had to stay strong for them. I was a solider, right?

"Can I hug my people before we pull off?" I asked the officers.

"Yeah, cause you gone be gone for a long time pal."

Although I was already in cuffs my mama hugged me and I kissed her on the cheeks and told her not to worry. My sister was in tears, I told her to be cool and get my money out my pocket and whispered in her ear to call JG, let em know what's up, take my car and go get the money out the safe and tell him to get me the best lawyer he can

." Love you. Get you a phone account set up so I can call."

"Okay bro keep ya head up."

"I'm good sis, hold it down for me." With that, we were on the way to jail.

JG

I had just received the call from Ronda telling me Darius got knocked. I had a feeling some funny shit was bout to happen because shit was going too good. It wasn't a doubt in my mind that Tugg was telling. This nigga been out for damn near a month but aint nobody seen him. Wasn't really no way they could charge D with any murder because there was only one witness and I damn sure wasn't gone open my mouth cause I knew if they had him they was probably looking for me. I told Ronda to tell him don't say shit to nobody and I would have his lawyer down there ASAP. Hopefully he could get a bond but it was highly unlikely. Long as he aint incriminate his self he would beat em. In the mean time, I had to hold down the operations. I started feeling too congested and watched in the projects so I found a house that was a double and opened up both sides of it for my crew. My partner was jammed up so I had to go two times harder. I just hoped that Drea was real and wasn't gone try no funny shit. I had to find Tugg to get his ass out of here.

<u>Drea</u>

"You have a collect call from Global Telling. To accept press 1."

"Hello."

"What up babe," he said.

"What happened?"

"I had warrant for two weeks for some bullshit ass murders."

"Oh my God are you..."

"Just listen, it's time for you to step up and be the queen you said you were. Continue to go to school and keep ya job. Somebody gone call you once a week or every other week to keep shit in order. I'm counting on you big time baby, Can you handle it?"

"Yes but"

"No buts"

"I'm a get a lawyer, beat this shit and be home soon. I may have to sit a minute but I'ma be cool. Just keep money on the phone and on my books and come see me when you can."

"Okay I got it, how am I supposed to get into the closet?"

"I'll let you know all that when you come see me. We can't talk over these phones like that."

"Okay keep ya head up and stay strong, I got us."

This was like Déjà vu to me. I seen it too many times, the only difference is these was murders, not drug charges. This is my chance to show this nigga I'm a bad bitch who bout her business. I'm a ride for mine like this nigga been riding for me.

DARIOUS

I sat in the block sick. I had no appetite, no words or nothing. It was hours before I spoke to anybody or even got off my bunk. Two murders and questioning for a third one…all I could see were these bitches bodies jerking every time the guns went off, and it played over and over in my head like a scratched CD. BOC…BOC…BOC…

And questioning for the another one? I was looking at a 180 do 90; I just knew it was over. Right when shit was getting good, but how? How the fuck they link me to this shit. Something wasn't right. We had on hoodies and mask when we killed the bitches and I didn't even pull the trigger at the club so can't nobody say I did shit.

It finally hit me, Tugg bitch ass was talking to the cops! Now it all made sense to me. After racking my brain for hours trying to figure shit out, I guess I ended up just passing out!

I woke up the next morning to the squads telling me I had an attorney visit, I couldn't have been happier. I hopped up and jetted out that mufucka. I got down stairs and seen an older black man whole looked to be in his mid to late 50s. He pointed to the chair and introduced himself as Martin Snyder.

"I was retained by Ronda Logan who claimed to be your sister, is that correct?"

"Yes sir."

"My fees are 30 thousand per murder if we go to trial and 20 thousand for the felony conspiracy. You are charged with will that be a problem?" "80 thousand? Are you guaranteeing that I walk free?"

"Nothing in this life world is guaranteed except for death Mr. Logan. I guarantee that I will give it all I got and that I am one of the best, if not the best criminal lawyer in the state of Indiana."

"Money not a problem, how much have they paid you already?"

"My retainer fee is 10 thousand per case and they gave me 25 to get started."

"Good I want a fast and speedy trial because they don't have any witness or evidence to find me guilty."

"Are you sure that's what you want to do, because I was gathering paperwork all night and they have a phone call recorded from a jail visit by a Tori Webster who I believe is a victim. In one account, a Shawn Tugglamore who appears to be the prosecutors C.I. I haven't heard the tape, but hearsay is enough for conviction so a fast and speedy trial may not be the best route for us to take."

Great way to start '07.

TUGG

Since I got out, I been all fucked up! I aint been able to find no type of rhythm out here, I can't sleep some nights, aint nobody been wanting to fuck with me on the work-tip and to make matters worse I been staying at Susie's house with her people and the baby trying to keep a low profile. She been stressing me clean the fuck out. She been acting like she know I got D knocked and saying slick ass shit bout me being broke and laying around her all day and asking me silly shit, like was I scared to go back to the apartments or am I hiding from somebody. I laugh it off but deep down it was making me want to back hand her ass for coming at me like that. I knew what was going on. I kept an ear to the street. I knew them niggas had 5 figures on my head, dead or alive, but I wasn't no fool. I figured with D locked up for 3 m's, JG would have his hands full handling business in the streets, so the last place he would look for me would be Susie's crib. I wasn't hiding or nothing, I was buying time, thinking of my next move. My biggest problem was having this bitch in my ear all day complaining about every fucking thing I did. I couldn't eat without her asking me "Do you gotta chew like that?" Between being dead broke and having a nagging ass bitch, I was losing my mind. The only things that could keep me sane were my son and the coke I had been coming across lately.

SUSIE

Hearing D had got locked up for murder had me very aggravated. He was supposed to be here for me; he was supposed to straighten out his situations and come back for me and my baby and get us away from here. He promised me that! Now he gone be gone? What am I supposed to do with this nigga and his baby.

I was starting to wish I had an abortion. Ever since Shawn got out, he been under me. I was forced to get a job so it works out cause he keep the baby but he been acting to damn weird. He be up all night not taking showers, smoking squares like they are not $5 a pack and just getting on my nerves. Q told me some niggas looking for him and got a $10,000 tag on em, but I made him promise that he wouldn't tell nobody he stayed here. I mean he is the father of my baby and even though he was a broke, dusty, lame ass nigga, the dick was fire and I know he still had potential to get me out the hood someday. The 10 Gs sounded good and I wanted to turn him in, but I couldn't because then I would have no one to depend on in the future.

CHAPTER 20

DARIUS

Jail felt like it was getting the best of me, they had me on meds for high blood pressure, I was taking other mufuckas med to go to sleep and the food was terrible. I was in the murder/robbery block, so every day I was seeing niggas getting sentenced to years they will never see. I was battling with my faith in God because I never went to church or prayed on the streets but this wasn't the streets. This was jail and niggas definitely prayed in jail. I would talk to my mother once a week and she would say pray every day, read the word and believe. So that's what I did.

As the weeks went by I started to become more social with the other inmates. The block held almost 90 people who were either fighting cases or going to the joint for more than likely at least a decade. More than half the guys were younger than 30 and most of them would sit around playing spades. Sometimes they would talk about the streets but most of em been fighting they case for so long that they had no way of communicating to the streets. They acted like they didn't care that they may not never go home. I stayed the-fuck away from them! I would sit at the chess table and watch the "O.Gs" of the block play chess. I didn't know how to play but I was catching on by watching them play game after game.

One morning after breakfast I was up looking at the news and one of the OGs who went by "Shep" asked me if I wanted to "push" a few games. "I never played before," I answered.

"You been watching us play for some time now, don't you pay attention?"

"Yeah, but I don't understand it all the way."

"It's like life youngster, you gotta think before you act and make the right decisions while protecting your people. Let me show you."

He taught me how to play and we became close. I told him I was charged with murder but didn't give any details. He told me he was back from the federal joint on an appeal that he was tryna give some time back or possibly get his case overturned. He encouraged me to get in the law library and learn all that I could about the charges I had because the system was crooked, even the lawyers.

I had started liking old man Shep because he was down to earth. He had been locked up the past 12 years and he knew a lot about all types of shit, so I found it easy to listen to him. He made me feel like if I had a father in my life, that's how he would be, like OG Shep, Full of wisdom and knowledge and sure of he he his.

One afternoon after we played numerous games of chess and I didn't win any. He said ,"You know why I like you D?"

"Why," I said.

"Because you aint like these other brothers your age. You got an old soul, you stay on top of them laws and you keep your mind focused on getting out. You do a lot of listening and not much talking and thats a good thing. It keep a mufucka wondering. I ain't gone lie young blood, I wonder about you myself. Not on no gay or nothing like that, but I wonder will you beat whatever they tryna pin on you and when you get back out there will you …"

"Hold up OG, you ain't got to even say that cause the only thing on my mind is being free." I cut Og off respectively.

"I feel that youngin but if it was that easy they would have been cut you lose, all I'm saying is look at every angle and be prepared for anything.

I felt what he was saying but going to the joint was not in my plans. I had started studying the law because I had a court date next week and learned they couldn't charge me with the Thanksgiving murders, so I wasn't really worried about that. The conspiracy was no more than 20 years, which was fucked up but more manageable than 120 years for the murders. I had been talking to Drea every day. Somedays, she would tell me to call back and we would talk for hours. She was out there holding shit down and doing her thang. Naturally I worried about her, but I knew she was smart so I didnt really trip. She came to see me on Valentine's Day and I was surprised to see her through the screen. "What up babe, I ain't know you was coming down here today."

"Boy, what you thought I would be doing? Chilling with another nigga?"

"Nah, at school or something."

"I took the day off to come see you, plus I'm moving."

"You moving?"

"Yeah, it's time for a change."

"Where you moving too?"

"I found a house out south, a two bedroom."

"Why two rooms?"

"We could use some space, it will be like an office. I told you we gone be legit babe, I been stacking all the money and focusing on my classes. I know you didn't really want to give me the combination to your safe so I took what you left out, flipped it and bought a new safe."

"You's a bad bitch!"

"The baddest nigga, get it right! Anyway I got a few ideas."

"What?"

"I don't want to do what I been doing. I want to do something different and focus on my school."

"Look, you smart and I believe you'll make the right decisions at the right time so do whatever you want to do as long as it's gone get us ahead. Anything you don't want to deal with, call lil bro and he will take it off your hands."

"Okay, how are you holding up in here?"

"I'm good, waiting to go to court. You talk to the lawyer?"

"No, I think your sister told him to call JG."

"Okay, tell that nigga I'm good, but I need to holla at him and he need to find ol boy."

"Okay I'm a call him when I leave, anything else you need me to do baby?"

"Yeah, keep that pussy wet for me, I'm coming home."

"Okay, love you." She blew me a kiss and the screen went blank. I went back to the block feeling good. I loved my bitch, she was holding it down fa' real.

JG

When I got the call from Drea, I was happy to hear my nigga was good. I had been on the lawyers trail, keeping him paid-up so I knew my nigga was coming home. I was impressed by Drea also, she wasn't the average hood bitch, she was game tight. When she told me she wanted to talk business I was a lil skeptical at first, but when she came to the double she had a glow about her that screamed money, she had a swag that demanded all the attention. Something about her was different. Most bitches be looking lost when they nigga get locked up but she looked like a woman on a mission.

"What up sis, you want to step in the back?"

"Yea, that's cool." WE went up-stairs.

"What's good, you cool?" "

Yeah, just tryna hold everything together till D get out."

"Okay, okay, that sound good, you need anything?"

"Well, I told him that I wasn't gone be out here selling dope like that because I need to foucs on school but I told him I'ma do something different."

"What you tryna do"

"I got a lot of family and know a lot of bitches that need weed so I'm a switch shit up, but I need a good connect," she said.

My hustlers ambition almost over rode my loyalty to my main man as I did the numbers quickly in my head but over charging her would be like robbing myself, so I looked out for sis. You know we all on the same team so I'm a give it to you how we get it, $7000 for an 11 pound bell. That's a lil less than $700 a pound. We sell pounds for a stack out of here and next door they bust them down and sell 25 dollars per quad to make $1600 per pound."

"Okay, right now I got 15,000 so let me get 2 bells and keep a G."

"You gone ride with it or you want it delivered."

"I'm a ride with mine." She stated boldly but sexy.

I had Unc put her shit in her car and she was gone. I was stunned. I knew it wasn't her money but for her to have the heart and brains to flip her dudes paper for him while he was fighting a murder charge had me mesmerized. I made a mental note to keep an eye on her just in case though, THESE HOES CAN NEVER BE TRUSTED!

In the meantime business was better than ever for me and my crew since we switched locations. We was making Peewee a fortune and half of the eastside was shopping with us because we had it for the low. Niggas was coming thru like it was a "free before 9" club. That was cool with me though because the more the merrier. It had been months since Tugg got out but no one seen the nigga. I wanted him dead on sight. Even though he couldn't point bro or me out, he was the only mufucka that could even link us to anything but his rat-ass was hiding good.

Chapter 23

DREA

_It felt good to have the power again, just like my daddy use to tell me, "When you got the money you got the power." I felt all those eyes on me in there, especially them two bitches. This the life I needed, I wasn't letting it go this time, that's why I wasn't fucking with no dope. When this nigga get out, he ain't gone want to sell dope either, we gone do shit right. I wanted the good life forever and the right cards were in my hand. I had to play it right. What Darius didn't know was that I took some of his money and paid a major down payment towards buying the house I told him about. I didn't know his money was coming in like it was till I had to take over for him. I figured he either got helly money in that safe or some money somewhere else because he was definitely getting it in! I may be wrong for taking it upon myself to get the fuck out here but if what I had planned out for us work out, that nigga gone be ready to put some ice on my fingers and hopefully some Juniors in my womb. If it don't, at least we will have a house almost paid for. Either way we were winning, so I had to get my grind on.

Chapter 24

DARIUS

_I had been locked up for over two months now and I was finally getting a chance to go in front of the judge. I was anxious. I knew they wouldn't be able to charge me with any murders without me saying anything about being on a scene because of the laws I had been reading. I was really worried about the conspiracy at the time. While I was in the bullpen waiting to be escorted in the courtroom, the deputy called me out and led me to the conference room. The room was fairly small and had a glass window separating me from the person on the other side. The lady who was on the other side reminded me of an older school teacher. She had glasses and looked very smart. "I am Lisa Frothers, the prosecutor for this courtroom, are you Mr. Logan?" she asked me.

"Yes maam."

"We would like to give you the chance to help yourself before we go in front of the judge. By doing so you will receive less time and be in the D.A.'s good graces." She said.

"Where is my lawyer at maam?"

"I don't know, that's not my job, my job is to find you guilty of these horrible crimes you've committed."

"I aint committed shit, why are we even in here?"

"I was sent to offer you this 80 year plea or give you a chance to do maybe 10."

"80? Man I aint got shit to say to you, I wanna talk to my lawyer." "Okay, that's your choice, don't say you didn't have a chance."

I could of spit through the glass on that bitch, tryna get me to talk. I was angry. They left me there for another ten minutes after she left and for the first time I wondered would I really beat these cases and go home one day or would I go to prison 4 ever?

When the deputy finally came to get me, my worried face turned to the game face. I couldn't show any signs of weakness in the courtroom. I walked into the courtroom all I could do was hold my head up high as I acknowledged my family, Drea, Susie and the baby. The judge read my charges out loud and asked me how I'd like to plead.

"Not guilty, your honor," my lawyer said. "Your honor, my client and I are asking that the courtroom dismiss the two counts of murder because of lack of evidence. It has been close to 90 days and the D.A. does not have anything or anyone that can say my client committed these murders."

"Does the state object?" the judge said.

"No sir, the state does not have any comments."

"The court agrees to dismiss both counts of murder due to lack of evidence.

"Thank you, your honor." I felt a lot of stress leave my body and heard my mother say "Thank you Lord" before the prosecutor spoke up.

"Your honor, Mr. Logan still has a felony for conspiracy for the murder of Jamal Tugglamore."

"How do you plead Mr. Logan?" The judge asked.

"My client pleads not guilty and would like for his bond to be reduced since the higher charges have been dropped."

"Object your honor, the state prefers for Mr. Logan to continue to stay in jail until the outcome of this case. He is being linked to two separate murders and is presumed to be a dangerous person. The state is willing to offer the defendant a 20 year suspend 10 in the DOC followed by five years of probation."

"Your Honor, my client has no intentions of singing any pleas or making any deals with the state. He's never been in any major trouble and he does not have any convictions on his record. He has a family to take care of that includes a new born your honor, so we are hoping for a bond reduction so that he may fight this from the streets."

"I will set the next court date for July 7th at 1:00 p.m. and grant Mr. Logan a $7500 charity bond." Just like that I was a free man!

CHAPTER 25

Back to the block I went. I knew it would be hours before my bond was posted but I wasn't tripping on that because I knew it was only a matter of time before I was back on the streets. I hollered at O.G. Shep for a while and he told me to get out and do something with my life. I told him I would and took his information after promising him I would look out for him.

It was almost 1 in the morning when the guards told me to pack up. This was the happiest I had been in a long time. Although it was only a few months it felt like forever. As I stepped out the garage of the jail, the winter weather of March never felt better to me. I took a deep breath and started walking towards the gas station to use the phone. Before I could take three steps I heard a familiar voice from a new blue Mustang. "You need a lift homeboy?" It was JG.

"How you know what time to be out here?" I said as I got in the sports car.

"I had the lawyer on it, you know we got to get our monies worth out his ass. We damn near 50 to the good with him."

"That 50 made it look good."

"What you thought I was gone break?"

"Not once, I just didn't want to see it happen like that."

"Yeah shit was starting to come together, but judging by this new whip it looks like shit still good?"

"Yeah, I'm a catch you up to everything."

"Aight, stop by the L first."

"I got you, but my nigga, business is beautiful out here! Me and my crew were moving 10-15 a month easily. The best move I could have made was getting out the hood. We got the whole east side on lock," "Drea been coming thru?"

"Naw she said she ain't want to sell dope without you being out here so she started grabbing pounds of the weed."

"Weed?"

"Yeah bro, she got to running through the shit so much I just introduced her to Diablo."

"Who the fuck is Diablo?" I asked puzzled.

"The plug, he good people bro. I got too much going on to be trying to keep everybody happy. Plus me and my crew ain't been fucking with no weed. The crack game is where it's at. Here."

He pulled out a bankroll that let me know shit was real.

"A lot can change in a few months!"

"I see. You seen Tugg bitch ass? I think he behind all this shit."

"Naw man, ain't nobody seen him but ain't a doubt in my mind he set this shit up. We got to a nice tag on his head."

"Yeah we got to get him, I guess that bitch Tori went to see him before she got hit up and described us to him and he put everything together just like we said was gone happen."

"The murders are dropped right?"

"Yeah but they recorded that tape and I think that's enough to find me guilty of this conspiracy, I don't know but I'm a fight it."

"What if we find him before trial?"

"Then we good!"

We pulled into the liquor store close to downtown. It felt great to breath fresh air again, a lot was on my mind but I felt free at the time.

JG went in to grab A bottle and I took the time to call Susie. I was surprised to see her at court, she was looking good. "Hello." She picked-up.

"What up baby girl?.....Hello?.....Hello?" I said.

Her line went dead.

She called back minutes later talking in a low voice. "Hello," she said. "What up, why you whispering?"

"I don't want to wake up the baby, he just went to sleep. Where you at?"

" I just got out a hour ago, I'm with bro at the L. What's up can I come over? "

"I don't wanna wake up this baby but mama can keep an eye on him and I can come out and meet you somewhere."

"Aight, meet me at LaQuinta Inn off the highway. I'm a be there in about 20 minutes."

"Okay, I'm headed out in a few; I love you and miss you."

"I love you too. I'm a see you in a minute."

JG came back to the car with a fifth of Grey Goose and a box of Swishers.

"Hope you got something to put in them Swishers, nigga." I joked.

He pulled out a sack of O.G Kush and said "I don't sell it no more but I keep a sack to smoke on."

"Drop me off at the LaQuinta, Susie bout to meet me up there," I said. "I thought you was coming to the spot with me and the crew."

"Naw, I need some pussy and I aint tryna be around Kia and Jazz off this drank. I might fuck up ya whole shit." We both laughed as we headed East on 465.

We pulled up to the lobby of the hotel and Susie's Sebring was already parked out front.

"Aight bro, right on for being on top of everything, I'm a catch up with you later on today after I get myself together."

"Aight nigga call me if you need me."

I got out and signaled for Susie to get out. She stepped out in her leggings and snow boots and came up and hugged me for like 5 minutes. I can't lie, she felt good in my arms and she was holding me like she was never going to see me again.

"Damn I miss you nigga," she said.

"I miss you too but let's get out this cold."

We went into the lobby and got a room.

"Damn it feel good to be free. Here roll up some of this bud, I need to smoke."

"So what the fuck happened D? You just moved out east and became fucking

Scarface. All I hear is how you and JG got everything on lock and how y'all killing everybody."

I had opened the fifth and started drinking like a fish, I laughed a lil at her comment because it was funny how mufuckas painted they own pictures of you.

"It aint nothing like that, it's really Tugg bitch ass talking to them people trying to save his ass and throw me and lil bro under the bus." "Shawn?"

"Hell yea, Shawn bitch ass!" I told her.

She passed me the smoke I passed her the bottle.

"What he got to do with it?"

"You know deep down that nigga really been jealous of a nigga, right?" "Uh huh." She mumbled.

"So some shit happened that involved some of his kinfolk."

"You talking bout Jamal, his babymama and her best friend?"

"Yeah, how you know?"

"It was all around the hood last year." she said.

"Yeah, so everybody saying we had something to do with it because they hate how we came up on em'. So I guess Tugg told police it was me who did everything and they locked my ass up."

"But that don't make no sense because how did Tugg know you had something to do with it?"

The liquor and smoke was getting the best of us and had us open. "That bitch Tori."

"Aint she the girl who got killed on Thanksgiving at the shop where I saw you and that "other bitch" at?"

"Yeah look, it's a long story but basically I was hollering at Tori the night her baby daddy got smoked and she told Tugg that the person who she seen do it was with me prior to shooting in the club."

"Right."

"So in the midst of all this, her and an innocent bystander get what they had coming for her running her mouth."

"So all this happened while Shawn was locked up?"

"Right, so this hoe ass nigga put the boys on me then go into hiding." "Is that why Q said it's a $10,000 tag on him?" "Hell yeah, have you seen him?

CHAPTER 26

SUSIE

I couldn't believe D had called me as soon as he got out. It had to be because of the baby. I had to sneak out because Tugg powderd- head ass was sure to be getting up from his cat nap. I was sick of this nigga! His habit had gotten so bad that he started doing the shit right in my face and was putting his hands on me more and more. Other than watching his son he had become worthless, his dick wouldn't even stay hard anymore, so when Darius called me I was up and out in no time. I felt kinda bad about not telling him the truth about the baby but this was my night to get my spot back and I was ready to please him any way I could. After smoking that kush and getting drunk as fuck, surprisingly, sex was not at the top of either of our to do lists. After he told me about his charges and how everything had happened I felt dumb as hell. How could I not have seen this shit? I had a feeling this nigga was sitting under me for a reason but I aint know how serious it was. My biggest concern was how would Darius look at me afterwards, but at the time the liquor had me not giving a fuck about too much and ready to tell this nigga how I felt.

CHAPTER 26 TRUTH HURTS

"Susie you alright"

"Huh? Yeah"

"Damn girl you just zoned out for a minute."

"Yeah I was just thinking."

"About what?"

"About us."

"What about us?"

"Darius, you know I love you and would do anything for you, why you leave me like that?"

"Man we ain't bout to go back through that shit, that's over and done with."

"You don't even understand," she began to cry.

"Understand what? Come here, what you crying for?"

"You don't know how much I really love you and what I been going though because of it."

"What you talking about? Having to raise the baby by yourself? I told you I had to get some shit straightened out first, I'm her now, we good ma."

"I'm sorry Darius," she started crying uncontrollably.

"We gone be alright baby, just talk to me, whatever it is we gone get through it, I promise."

"You promise."

"On my life, just keep it 100 with me."

"Okay, I know where Shawn is."

"What!"

"I know where he at right now."

"Where?"

"In my bed."

"Huh?" I was dumbfounded.

"What you mean he in ya bed, you been fucking that nigga?"

"Yes."

"You left him there with my son?"

She opened the floodgates and let all her tears come out.

"He's not yours..."

"Bitch what?"

"I'm so sorry Darius."

"Who's is he then?"

'Shawn's."

I was angry and hurt. I felt crossed and betrayed but a lil relieved. I rolled up another blunt, got high, drank some more as I watched her cry and try to explain herself for 20 minutes.

"I...I was just ...lost and...mad at you.. And he was telling me bullshit about how... How you was out there fucking all those bitches and was using me..."

I had enough of her sob story.

"Using you for what Susie? You let this nigga game you ma, I aint mad though, not at him at least. I'm mad that you would lie to me about a whole a baby- situation, fuck that, the fact that you was fucking him! I'm a real nigga and you don't treat real nigga like that."

"I know, I'm sorry, how can I make it up to you?"

"We a figure something out."

I had enough for one day, I was fresh out from two murder charges and shit was already stressing me out! I was glad I knew where Tugg was but the nigga in me was shitty that my bitch played me like that. I was kinda wishing I had just went home and those thoughts lead me to thinking about Drea.

She held shit down for me the whole time I been gone, but I was out now and didn't even know where the new house was. I started wondering if she knew I was out. What would she do if she knew I was here with this bitch? I should call her up here to beat this bitch up! A million thoughts were going through my head as I sat in the room drunk then a bitch.

"Look we gotta get some shit straight first, under no circumstances do you ever lie to me again about anything."

"I won't, I promise I won't."

"You gone help me get Shawn too."

"You gone kill him?" She whisperd.

" I aint gone do it, but it's gone get done."

"What about my baby Darius? I know I was wrong but he is my child's father. I'm only telling you this because I love you with all my love. I trust you and believe you when you tell me shit. I feel like it's supposed to be me and you like it used to be. I can't see myself living without you D."

"I feel you, but shit change ma, we were teenagers when we started fucking around, we grown now."

"What that mean?"

"I'm just saying man, you know I got a girl right now and I'm happy with her."

"If you so happy with her, why you here?"

"Because I thought you was my baby mama but obviously everything we had was a lie."

"Don't say that because you know that's not true."

"Okay, not everything! But fuck it, it is what it is, you want to fuck with me you gone have to accept me as is just like I'm accepting you and your baby."

"And what exactly does that mean?"

"That mean if you keep it 100 with me and help me out, I will always be there for you and yours long as I can."

"You promise?"

"I promise. Now come here, you know I aint had no pussy in months." She seductively kissed me all over and we had drunk sex till the morning.

CHAPTER 27

We woke up the next morning hung over a little. I wasn't letting that phase me because I had a lot of shit to take care of. I had Susie drop me off at JG spot and told her I would call her later. We planned to get Tugg ASAP and even though she seemed scared I think she was down. I had JG take me to the barbershop and the mall. I called Andrea and told her to meet me at JGs a hour later. It felt good to take a shower and get fresh. I was starting to feel like my old self.

"What's up sexy?" Kia said to me as I walked into the living room where the crew was "Welcome home."

"Right on, right on, I'm glad to be here. I been hearing nothing but good news. I tip my hat to y'all."

"You know we hold shit down big homie."

"Let me holla at you in the back bro," I said to JG, I still didn't feel comfortable talking business around his crew and I could tell by the looks on their faces that they didn't like that but, I had to be extremely careful after this shit I just got out of. We walked to the back room, "What up bro?" "Nigga I got the drop on Tugg!"

"Straight up?" He asked sounding surprised.

"Yeah"

"Where he at?" I didn't wanna tell him but I had to.

"Man, that nigga been hiding at Susie house."

SSusie house? What the fuck he doing over there? They related?"

"Em-Em, that's, that nigga baby." I mumbled.

"Get-the-fuck-outta-here, you bullshitting!"

"I swear to God, the bitch told me everything last night."

"Scandalous ass bitch, that grimy ass nigga, he gotta go ASAP."

"I know bro"

"You want her gone too? If she cross him it's only a matter of time before she cross you. Knowing you, you probably done told her too much anyway."

"Why you say that?"

"I know you bro, that's just you, you put a lot of trust in these bitches sometimes, look at ya situation with Drea, and you left her with some bands, what if she ran off with ya shit?"

"Come on bro, not right now. Plus she on her way now."

"I'm just saying bro; Susie might be a problem down the road. We can nip it in the bud now!"

"Nigga I just got two murders dropped and fighting a conspiracy for yo ass lil bro! we can't just keep killing mufuckas."

"Nigga last time I checked you aint killed a mufucka ! Nigga I'm doing this shit for you, nigga for us! This the life we chose D, don't forget nigga! Did you like sitting in there listening to the niggas stunt and dick-ride half the city and all the rap industry? Nigga, that's what it gone be if we let these mufuckas start running they mouth, remember that!" He stormed out and left me alone thinking about my situation. I was broken out of my trance by my phone ringing.

"Hello?"

"I'm outside."

"Oh right, here I come." I walked back to the front, told he crew I would catch up with them and told JG "Be ready." I was all in. the streets had me, I felt trapped. I was taking this shit personal now because bro was right. This nigga was running his mouth bout some shit he aint know nothing about. He had to get dealt with.

CHAPTER 28

Once again I was feeling like my life was in the hands of someone else. This shit was getting crazy it was like the deeper I got into the game the more I wanted to get out of it. I was more than happy to see Drea. She had a new car, had on air maxes instead of heels, and just had a whole different demeanor about herself. I sat next to her and just admired her for a minute. I seen a different kind of beauty in her today, it may have been I just was locked up for a minute but she wasn't the same Drea I had left out here.

"You just gone stare or you gone give me a kiss and a hug?" She said showing her pretty smile.

"Damn my bad you just look different."

"Is that good or bad?" she blushed.

"Nah, nah, not anything bad, it's like a sexy glow type of look, come here." We kissed passionately before pulling off.

"So what you been out here doing? I see you got you and whip and shit, where my cars at?"

"Just sit back and enjoy being free for a minute, all your questions will be answered shortly. You tell me why am I just now seeing you if you been out long enough to get a haircut and go to the mall or wherever you went too?"

"Oh, I had bro come scoop me up when they let me out and he took me to get fresh, I aint want you to see me like that."

"Nigga run that lame ass line on that whack ass baby mama of yours that was at court. Who you think I am Darius? I know when the fuck you got out and I got a feeling that

I know who the fuck you was with all night. Now do you wanna be a man or let this be the point of our relationship where we start lying and hiding shit from each other?"

I was speechless, not only did I feel dumb for trying to spin her like she wouldn't be the one calling the jails to see when I actually got out, but I was thinking about what she said about fucking our relationship up. "Your right babe."

"I know."

"But its deeper than what you thinking."

"Okay, I'm sure it is but why you couldn't just call me? Nigga I'm out here risking my life and my future for us and you aint even man enough to keep it real with me, boy when you gone start being a man? I'm doing everything I can for us and this how you repay me? Go fuck a bitch who probably would've never bothered to tell you about your child? That's the type of woman you would choose over me?"

"Naw baby, you tripping."

"You did it last night."

"But it wasn't like that."

"Well how the fuck was it, because my man was released from jail almost 12 hours ago and I'm just now seeing him. Nigga I'm supposed to be top priority before mama, before JG and definitely before THAT BITCH! You're not going to keep playing with me like this."

We were on the highway and she was in tears. I was feeling bad for choosing to call Susie instead of Drea but what else could I say? Players fuck up! I had to get control of the situation.

"Look Andrea, you my girl, you wifey. If I would of got knocked on them cases you would of ended up with everything. I called her because while I was down all I could think about was getting my life together and at the top of that list was my son. Other than getting that part of my life together, I'm ready to start them business plans and get our life on point."

"How you tryna get our lives together if you fucking that bitch D. I can understand the shit about the baby but you stayed with her all night and left me lonely another night."

"That's because we got to drinking and talking bout some shit until I passed out."

"So y'all didn't fuck?"

"Naw I was too shitty."

"Huh, really?"

"For real"

"Shitty for what?"

"Well for one she been lying to me about the baby."

"I knew it! Trifling-ASS- bitch!"

"Yep, but that aint the worst part, Tori's dude Jamal had a cousin named Tugg who use to be my nigga. Well he the nigga who behind a lot of this shit and he the nigga who put my name with the murders to the police."

"Okay sooooo, what he got to do with Susie?"

"That's who's baby she had."

"What-the-fuck, are you serious?"

"Yep, but not only that we been had on tag on the nigga head and he been staying at this bitch house."

"This some Jerry –Maury type shit, now I'm caught up in ya little love triangle."

"I told you, I had a lot going on from the jump, you the one who swore you was down to ride."

"I still am I just want you to be honest with me about everything." We were finally off the highway and pulling up to a nice ranch-style home with a garage and fenced in yard. The driveway sat my Monte Carlo.

"Welcome Home!"

"Who helped you find this place, it's nice."

"Boy, you aint even seen the inside."

We got out and went in through the side door. She had it all laid out. Flat screens on the wall and office room with a computer and desk in it. Our bedroom had new everything.

"What the fuck have you been out here doing?"

"I took the money and the rest of the stuff you left and invested in weed."

"Weed got us living like this?"

"Yeah but come here."

She lead me to the den closet and popped out a safe-wall where 2 safes sat behind it.

"I figured you would want something to come home too, that's why I never asked for your combination, but the one on the left is ours, the combination is 24, 8, and 30."

I opened it and saw a nice bundle of money and some pounds of weed. "It's close to 15 Gs I hope you aint mad at me."

"Why would I be mad?"

"Because the look on your face is like there's a nice chick of cash somewhere."

"That did cross my mind."

"I put it down on this house."

"How much they want for it?"

"65"

"You did all this with weed?"

"Yeah, ya brother got tired of me having to go through him every other day so he gave me Diablo number, he started of charging me $7000 a bell but I guess my charm and good looks made him wanna drop the price to $5500 for me."

"He be flirting with you?"

"Of course."

"Has he tried to fuck?"

"Don't start that BS Darius, you either gone trust me or you aint, I aint no whore or slut like you. I'm just playing. Come in here so we can break this bed in."

She slid off her 95s and led me to the bedroom. I started kissing on her and undressing her at the same time. "Damn I miss this sexy ass body." "Show me you miss it," I kissed her from top to bottom before taking my time to use my tongue as a navigation to her womanhood. I was getting more and more passionate as she getting more and more wet. "I'm bout to cum, I'm bout to cum." She started moving to a type of rhythm with her hand controlling my head before arching her back and squirting out cum like she had a mini gun inside her. While she started playing with herself I took the time to strip down to nothing and go inside her with every inch I had. She rolled me over and started riding me, I felt like I was on top of the world. I sat up and started sucking on her titties and kissing all on her neck and she pushed me back down and started grinding even harder on me. "I'm bout to cum again, cum with me!" she moaned in the sexiest voice I ever heard. I looked up and seen her eyes rolling hard and that made me release everything I had in her. As she laid on my chest I could still feel wetness running down her thighs.

"Damn, I needed that girl."

"If you would of came home last night you would of gotten more than that but I'm putting you on a punishment."

"Ha-Ha you silly, you aint gotta worry about me baby, I'm gone always come home sooner or later."

"Can you promise me one thing?" she asked.

"What?"

"That you don't kill nobody else." I want you and I need you here with me every night."

"Sometimes a man gotta do what a man gotta do."

"I feel if its life or death but this shit you in right now, let your brother and his crew take care of them."

"Who is them?"

"That bitch and her nigga."

"What make you think I wanna kill her?"

"That bitch is scandalous baby, don't get me wrong. I don't condone to just killing people but this is a different scenario, that bitch was gone use you for as long as she could, just so happen she got caught in her deceitful ways. It's only a matter of time before she try to set you up if she willing to set-up her own baby daddy.

I will kill that bitch myself before I let her get you."

"You would do that for me?"

"Anything for mines."

"How you know she tryna set dude up for me?"

"I know how bitches like her think and I know my man."

"You a trip."

"Whatever, I need to know that you gone let them handle that, cause I don't want you not here with me, JG got all them mufuckas around him for a reason and my daddy use to always tell his top workers that Ain't no need to have soldiers if you aint gone use them. "

I was starting to feel like me doing that little time was a blessing in disguise because it seemed like shit was just falling in place all of a sudden. I had a girl that seemed like she just wanted to see me happy and wanted the best for me. I know where the enemy was laying his head at night, I had a house that was mine and I had close to 50 Gs to my name. Other than the case and wondering about how to deal with Susie, I was living a lot better than before.

CHAPTER 29

TUGG

This "Laying low" shit was getting played out. This bitch don't wanna give me no pussy no more, this baby been driving me crazy crying all the damn time and this hoe ass nigga Q been hiding his work somewhere that's not in this damn house. I done searched this mufucka high and low several times. I'm waking up in the middle of the night sweating and shit, dozing off and getting up cause the baby crying and this bitch be gone. I don't know what the fuck going on but I know this monkey on my back got me frustrated and I need to get out and get some air. I don't even know where this bitch at now but when she bring her black ass home I'm taking her car keys.

SUSIE

After I dropped Darius off I headed home feeling relieved. I got the truth out, got some good dick and I was getting a chance to show him how much I love him. It's amazing how real niggas can make you feel. Now I just had to figure out how I was gone get this nigga out the house because I sure in hell want gone turn my mamas house to nobody's crime scene. As I walked into the house I was surprised to see him up with the baby. "Hey boo, the baby must've woke you up?"

"Bitch don't try that lovey dovey shit with me, where the fuck you been all morning?"

"I had to run some errands for the baby and for my mama."

"Look like you been getting fucked all night, come here."

He snatched me up by the arm and started sniffing me like I was a bud of weed.

"Bitch I smell that liquor through your pores."

SMACK! He opened handed me.

"Why the fuck you lying, where you been?"

"I just had a few drinks." SMACK!

"You a fucking unfit mother."

"What the fuck are you?" The last smack knocked me down and had my nose bleeding but I was so pissed off, I got up and was talking shit to him. "What type of nigga are you? You don't do shit for ya self!"

I was crying tears of anger and rushed him, he grabbed me and slammed me on the living room floor, "Bitch you think you better than me or something?" SMACK. A backhand across my face again. The baby start crying as he mounted his body on mine and pinned my arms down, I was helpless, "Bitch you wanna sneak out and go get fucked while I'm sleep but don't wanna give me none of this pussy" SMACK!

He smacked me again and it knocked all the fight out of me, I just laid there crying, I couldnt even find the strength to fight him.

"I guess I'm a have to take it." He bragged.

He ripped off my shirt and bra and yanked my leggings down,

"Nigga, you gone rape me in front of our son?"

"Shut yo sluttish ass up." SMACK.

I Couldn't even cry no more I was just ready for it to be over,

"Bitch turn over I don't wanna look at yo nasty ass face!"

He forcefully turned me over and rammed his dick in my ass and crammed me until he saw blood.

"Yeah bitch now yo ass bloody, just like yo face. Where the fuck your keys at?"

I was in so much agony that I couldn't even move, he grabbed the keys and left me and the baby crying. After ten or so minutes I got up and got my baby to stop crying and ran me some bath water. I sat my son in the bathroom in his walker as I sat in the hot salt water thinking about what had really just happened. Tears rolled down my face as the whole scene replayed in my head.

I grabbed my phone and called Darius.

"What up Susie." He said after he answeard.

"He beat me up and raped me D!" Soon as I heard his voice I just burst out crying.

"He beat you up and raped you?"

"Yeah."

"Why?"

"I don't know I just came in the house, he started questioning me and telling me I smelled like sex and liquor and just started smacking me." "And he raped you?"

"Yep, right in front of my son!"

"where he at now?"

"He took my keys and left, he can't be nowhere except for the apartments."

"Okay, get yourself together and call if he come back."

"Okay, I love you."

"Love you too!!" Click up.

CHAPTER 30

TUGG

Damn, I don't know why the fuck I just did that girl like that, I was tripping. I done beat this bitch up, raped her and took her car but I aint got have nowhere to go. I needed a bag bad but I aint have no money. I thought about going back and taking her purse but I couldn't go back right now, I felt bad. I headed to the only place I could, the hood! The hood gone always love me. I aint been out here in some months, everything still looked the same though except it was a lot of new faces. All I needed was to find one of my niggas who could front me something and help me get back on my feet, but it seemed like I aint know nobody I saw. I could go to Mimi's house where I know everybody be at, but I aint want everybody to see me. She had tinted windows so I wasn't worried about being seen by anybody I didn't want to be seen by.

I parked backwards by the b-ball courts and had to wait on an victim; somebody was gone give me a bag of powder or buy me a bag! I sat parked for about 25 minutes thinking of a plan before I saw a couple bad bitches sitting on the benches watching their niggas play ball. After another 10-15 minutes they were walking towards the apartment buildings where I was parked. These hoes looked like they had at least enough for me to get a gram. I had to get them.!

I let down the window and hollered at them. Aye what y'all doing round here?"

"We just out here visiting our cousin."

"Who y'all cousin?"

KKeatha in building 3, you know her?"

"Yeah, I know everybody out here, I run these apartments."

"WWhat's ya name?"

"Everybody round here call me king. Y'all tryna go get something to eat. It's on me?"

"Yeah we aint doing nothing else." "Hop in."

CHAPTER 31

JG

"That nigga did what? ah, he tripping we got them though,"

I was shocked to hear that. Tugg done raped this bitch. When he told me he took her car I knew this was the perfect opportunity to get his ass. I called my main crew out the party room for a meeting.

"This nigga done came out of hiding y'all. "

"Where he at?"

"We don't know exactly where he at but he done beat his bitch up, raped her and took her car. He probably aint got no money or nowhere to go so 9 times outta 10 he gone end up in the hood sooner or later. Keith and Kevin, I'm a send y'all out there in some hooping gear but y'all keep them thangs ready cause he dead on sight. Jazz and Kia I want y'all to put on something real sexy that's guaranteed to make a nigga double look and say something to y'all and that's when y'all work that magic on him. "How we gone know what he look like?"

"Just look for a nigga who looking a lil rough in a purple Sebring. Everybody know how important this is to the team so move smooth." With that, everybody got they shit together and cut out. After about 45 minutes, I received a text, "I'm in the backseat, and Kia is in the front. He think he taking us out to eat."

I replied, "Try to get him to Unc's spot on 27th, are you sure it's the right nigga?"

She texted back "yeah, he look rough and sound desperate."

"Okay y'all be careful and call me if anything go wrong," I texted back. "Where we going King? Jazz asked him.

"I don't know it's up to y'all."

"Let's stop at the gas station first to get some blunts, do you smoke?" "Hell yeah y'all already got some weed?"

"Yeah just some cool reggie, it aint no Kush or Purp but it gets you high."

"I usually keep a fat sack on me, I was really just waiting on my nigga to hit me back," he lied as he turned in to the CITGO and pulled up to the pump.

"Y'all got some change to grab the blunts, I aint got nothing smaller than a dub."

"Kia, go grab a box of blunts and an orange juice."

"Grab me a box of Ports too, I'll hit u back." Tugg said.

Kia got out the Sebring and gave Tugg something to watch as she headed in the store.

"Damn, did y'all say y'all were rela....AGGHHH – bitch-what the fuck."

Being too focused on Kia and her fat ass had Tugg off his square and feeling a pain shoot through his body that made him loose total control of everything and black out. Kia made it back to the car and was lost for a second. "Girl, what the fuck happened, he tried you?"

"Nah, I tazed his bitch ass till he blacked out soon as you got out the car. Now go back in there and buy some black tape so we can tie him up and throw him in the back. We gone meet JG at Unc's.

Kia went in the store, got the tape and came back to help Jazz. After struggling for a few minutes they had his arms tied together and had him leaned back in the passenger seat with the seatbelt on. It was a few people looking in the car from other pumps but that didn't faze them, they were on the clock. Jazz hopped behind the wheel, and Kia climbed into the backseat as they pulled off. After a 20 minute drive Jazz called JG, "We bout to pullup."

"Pullup in the back, is he dead?"

"Naw, he just blacked out."

"Okay, we a be there in no time. Go knock on the door and help Unc get him in the basement."

"PSSSST" 'Ah man, what the fuck was that, where the fuck am I?" Tugg screamed as the fire from the Newport burnt his arm. "You in hell, pussy!" Kia said in an evil tone. Still dazed and trying to come to, Tugg opened his eyes and damn near had a heart attack as he adjusted them to the darkness.

"D, JG, what the? How I get here? You niggas kidnapped me?"

"Damn my nigga you don't seem happy to see us?"

"How the fuck did I get here??" D yelled for the girls and they came down smoking a blunt.

"Remember them?" he asked.

"Fake ass bitches!" Tugg said, as he looked up. He shook his head feeling defeated.

"Yeah nigga, hollering at every bitch you see done cost you ya life." "Man is this what this is all about? Susie? Nigga you gone kill me over a bitch?"

"Jazz, burn that nigga with the blunt."

"Aww fuck D, come one man."

"Nigga aint you had enough of disrespecting the ladies in they face." "Man my bad just let me go please man, what you want? You want me to stay away from her?"

"Man, just tell me why Tugg, why you have to cross me? Nigga I kept it 100 with you from day one."

"It was her D, on my life. She kept pushing up on me tryna give me the pussy. I told her it wasn't right but she kept throwing it at me." He pleaded.

"Then she got pregnant and was tryna put the baby on you!"

"Nigga you don't get it do you?" D said. "Nigga, you bout to die and all you can think about is some pussy you should've never fucked. Nigga that's my bitch and always gone be mine, you just wanted to be me so bad that you was willing to cross a real nigga over some pussy. I can understand that but this shit deeper than that! I wouldn't kill a nigga over fucking my bitch, but I will kill a nigga for being a snitch!" Tugg eyes got big as fuck and piss started running down his leg.

"Nigga don't get scared and piss on yourself now, you wasn't scared when you were raping your baby mama nigga."

"Nigga fuck you, you think you a boss out..." POW!

He never got to finish his last word. The single shot to the dome took his life. D sat there with the 9 still smoking as he held it.

"That nigga was getting too disrespectful, JG have Unc clean this shit up and get this nigga outta here. One of y'all ride with me to get this girl her car back."

"What you gone do about her?" asked JG.

"I'm a handle her!" Kia grabbed the keys and her and D headed out. "Roll up." I passed her a sack.

"Where we going?" Kia asked.

"We gone take her car back in a minute but I need to clear my head first."

"You don't really wanna kill her do you?" she asked as she was rolling the weed.

"You don't even want her dead do you?"

"Damn is it written on my face?"

"Naw, I just been paying attention to shit, and me being a female I can tell you still love her."

"I don't love her; I got love for her though."

"Is it a major difference?"

"Yeah, cause when you in love you do almost anything for a mufucka but when you just love a person it don't be that deep. You might not understand, I don't never see you or Jazz with no niggas other than the click."

"Because niggas aint shit and we bout our cash. But this aint about us, this about you and your lil bitch."

"I know, I can't just have her killed, what about her baby?"

"D, you ever feel like this life just aint for you? You a different type of dude than most street niggas."

"Hell yeah, all the time."

"Yea, you seem like the family type. Maybe in another life you would make the perfect husband."

"Whaaaaat? Let me find out you tryna go soft on us."

"Nah, I'm just keeping it real, sometimes I wish I had a lil family and you seem like you would be a good dad." The weed had her open.

"I'm human so of course this pussy get wet and I crave for some dick at times but aint to many niggas worth me giving myself too."

"Can I ask you a question Kia?"

"What"

"How many niggas you been with?"

"What you mean by been with?"

"Fucked!"

"Only two different niggas, 3 times all together."

"Why you and Jazz choose this lifestyle? Everybody know it's only two ways out."

"The same reason you choose it, we like nice shit! Nigga, where you driving too?"

The blunt went out and they were just riding through the city.

"I don't know my head fucked up a lil right now."

"I got something for you." She pulled out his dick and started sucking it as he drove.

"I knew you wanted some of this dick!" he moaned out as he looked down at her head in his lap.

"Nigga, pay attention to the road." She said while coming up for air. After busting the nut all in her mouth, they found their selves parked in from of Susie crib.

"What you got planned."

"I got another spot I'm a let her post up in till I get shit figured out." "You sure you don't want me to just run in there and kill her?"

"Naw get in the back, she bout ride with us."

"Aight, but what me and you do is between us."

"Come on baby girl, I know." He said as he got out the car.

KNOCK, KNOCK, KNOCK Susie opened the door and burst out crying when she saw D standing there. He hugged her, "Go get your baby and come on."

"You know she gone think something going on with us don't you?" Kia said as D got back in the car.

"I'm a real life player Kia, welcome to the team."

"You need a bitch like me don't you? That head was only a sample." "You crazy, just play by the rules, no funny shit."

"I got you!" By now Susie was opening the passenger door and letting the seat up to put her baby and the car seat in.

"Hi, um D who is this in my backseat?"

"I'm Kia."

"Just put the baby in the car and lets go, I'm a explain everything." She got in, "I got a place up north for you and lil homie. The rent paid up for a few months but I'm a pay it for another year. I'm a help you get on your feet.

"Okay who is Kia?"

"That's my friend, she gone help us do whatever need to be done.

CHAPTER 32

Back on 27th

"Man hurry up and roll that nigga in the carpet." JG screamed at Keith and Kev. Everybody was getting nervous because sirens could be heard in the neighborhood. "What we gone do when we get him rolled up?" "We gone put him on the truck and have Unc ditch his ass."

"Nigga I know you hear them sirens out there, they getting closer and closer."

"Nigga they out here every day who's to say they coming for us?" Jazz came running down the steps.

"They out there two cars deep parked in the driveway."

"Fuck, alright, don't panic! Jazz and Unc, y'all stay upstairs and try to keep them from coming in."

"What we gone do." Asked Kev

"Stay down here with me."

"Nah everybody upstairs but me" said Unc.

"You sure?" JG said. He looked in Unc eyes and could tell he was tired of his life. "Yea, if anybody go down for this body its gone be me. Did D take the gun?"

"Naw here wipe if off." He passed Unc the 9 and they went upstairs. BOOM BOOM BOOM, the police banged on the door.

"We know someone is in there, open the door. "It's IMPD!" they turned on the TV and cut its volume up before getting comfortable looking.

"Open the door Jazz, nobody answer any questions." Jazz opened the door and 2 armed cops were standing on the other side with their guns drawn.

"Let me see your hands!" they screamed. Jazz lifted both arms, "Back-step into the house next to them. How many people in here? Asked one of the officers.

No one said anything, by now back-up had arrived and the house was turning into a crime scene. JG, Kev, Keith and Jazz were all cuffed as the officers, searched the house. It was less than 10 minutes before they heard a gunshot from downstairs. JGs head immediately dropped and a single tear rolled down his face. Unc was the ultimate OG who had been through everything already. We knew he had just given up his life or freedom for the team. POW! Another round let off as the other officers ran down to see what was going on.

"Dispatch we have three DOAs on 27th and Carrolton and an additional four detainees. We are going to need a wagon and a few trucks." Meanwhile, me, Kia and Susie was in the spot up North I had sis get me. I hadn't been here since I got out. "This is a nice apartment said Kia." "Who stay here?"

"Only people that know about this place is us three and my sister. Susie, you gone stay here until further notice."

"Are we gone get some furniture?"

"Yeah." I went to the safe that was there and opened it, thinking Sis had cleaned me out. To my surprise it was just as I left it. I gave them $7500 and told them to spend it all on the house. "I'm a go handle some other shit and come back to get y'all in a lil bit. Kia is here to help you so you don't be all stubborn and stuck up. She my peoples, y'all should get along good." I left them there with the baby and headed out South.

CHAPTER 33

I drove home feeling more free but something still felt wrong. I tried calling JG but his phone went to voicemail, I wasn't worrying bout him I know he'd call when he got everything on point. I pulled up to the driveway and went into the house and heard the shower running and heard Mary J's CD playing on blast. I slid out my gear and headed straight to the bathroom.

She was a little startled when the shower curtain opened. "Boy don't be sneaking up on me like that." She said.

I took off my socks and boxers and got in with her. The hot water felt extra relaxing running down my body. She hugged me from the back and told me to loosen up. "Whatever happened in the streets, leave it there, you with me and this is our time." She began to massage my shoulders and reach down and around to my 3rd leg. "Somebody happy to see me." She said as she stroked my solider making it stand to full attention. It aint even 3:00 yet and my day been long as fuck already," I said, as I turned to her, grabbed her ass cheeks and begin sucking her titties. I had her back against the shower wall and bend up her pussy while the other one was holding her leg up. “Put it in,” she whispered in my ear as she kissed and nibbled on down my neck. I went up in her and felt pure pleasure. It was kinda hard to find proper footing, so I turned her around, bent her over and long stroked her from the back. The pussy was feeling good but Kia kept popping up in my head for some reason. I was wondering if her pussy felt better than this.

After cumming all up in her wetness I washed up and left her in there. I went to get dressed and heard my phone beeping indicating that I had a message. I checked it and had 12 missed calls from the county. What the fuck? Who's locked up I thought to myself. Then the phone rang again.

"Hello."

"You have a collect call from JAZZMINE." I immediately pressed 0 to accept.

"What up Jazz, What happened?"

"They popped up at the spot on 27th and locked everybody up for murder."

"Who is everybody?"

"Me, JG, Kev, and Keith." "Where Unc?"

She paused briefly.

"I think him and a police officer killed each other. They was in the basement with Tugg and we were all upstairs."

"Tugg dead too?"

"Yeah."

"Okay don't talk to nobody and sit tight, call me later."

"Okay, where Kia?"

"She with me."

"Tell her I love her." 'Aight." I was hurt, not only was my crew gone, Unc was dead and it was all on me. I got dressed and told Drea and it was all my fault. She had ran her some bathwater and was looking real comfortable. She didn't question me or nothing, she asked me to bring her a glass of wine, a blunt, and to replay her Mary J.

CHAPTER 34

I hopped back on the highway in a trance. Unc was dead. Tugg was dead and my brother and his crew were locked up for murder. A thousand thoughts were going through my head. I was wondering if Kia already knew. I hoped she did cause I aint' wanna be the one to have to tell her. I walked into the apartment and was surprised to see Kia holding the baby while Susie was sleep on the floor.

"How long she been sleep?" I asked.

"About 30 minutes, you talk to ya bro yet?"

" Naw I talked to Jazz though. They all got locked up at the house."

"For what?" She cried.

"She said they were charged with murder."

"No! She can't go to jail. That all I got out here. Can they charge all them with murder? How did the police find out?" she cried.

"Just chill out Kia, everything gone be okay, we gone get them a lawyer and they gone beat it like I beat mine."

"What am I gone do without them, Darius."

"You good ma, you can stay here with Sue and we gone get everything straightened out I swear."

"I knew something was going on cause somebody kept calling from a jail number but I don't have an account set-up, so I couldnt answer." "Don't worry we gone get everything on point." Susie had woke up towards the end of the conversation.

"Shawn dead too?" she looked me in my eyes and asked.

"Yeah, he gone," I replied confidently.

"This aint the time to beat ourselves up, we all gotta step up and help each other right now. Kia I need you to call and see what everybody's bond is and set up an account on your phone. Susie, get the baby together and lets go get some shit for the spot."

We all packed in the Sebring and went shopping for furniture. The shopping took a lot of pressure off all of us and lightened up the mood. Kia and Susie were getting along fine while I was trying to get in contact with Mr. Snyder. His secretary told me she would have him call me ASAP. I called Drea to kill some time.

"What up baby? You still at the crib?"

"Yeah, I'm doing some extra credit work online, then I got a few places to go, what you doing?"

"Trying to get in contact with the lawyer, JG and his crew got locked up earlier."

"For what?"

"Murder."

"Oh, God, did you have anything to do with it Darius?"

"Nah, I'm good."

“Okay, when you gone be home, I miss you already?”

“ I’m a be there later after I get shit handled.”

“Okay baby be careful, love you!”

“Love you too!”

The lawyer called after I hung up with Drea. “Hello.”

“Hi, how are you Mr. Logan?”

“I’m good, I need you though.”

“What’s up, you catch another case?”

“Nah, my partners did though.”

“What kind of case if it?”

"4 people charged with murder, confinement and visiting common nuisance."

"4 people?"

"Yeah they need to be bailed out immediately."

"Okay I'm a get on it; I'll give you a call later."

"Okay." He hung up.

I waited another 20 or so minutes before they came out the furniture store. They were all smiles. "What y'all so happy for," I asked them. "We went over our limit."

"Y'all spent more than 7,500 in there?"

"Yeah it came up to about 9 grand, Kia paid the rest."

"What the fuck y'all get?"

"You a see" said Kia, I think you gone like it, they gone deliver in the next couple hours so we gotta get back."

I dropped them off and went downtown to the lawyers' office.

"Come on Mr. Logan." He said. After having me wait for several minutes. "Have a seat." He sounded serious.

"This case is more complicated than what it seems,"

"What you mean by that?"

"First of all, with the victim being Shawn Tugglamore, I don't think it would be wise for me to represent any of them while your case is pending. We wouldn't want any type of contradictions through association."

" I see what you saying, that would make sense." I replied.

" And on top of that Jamar Gaines aka JG is part of an Federal investigation!"

"What you mean."

"Apparently the feds have been watching him for the past few months on unrelated charges."

"What kind of charges?"

"Cocaine."

"Okay, so do you think they on to me?"

"Well his phone probably was tapped so I don't know, all I can say is switch all your numbers and still watch what you say on the phone. If he is given a bond, don't be so quick to pay it cause the feds may hold him."

"Okay what about the other three?"

"I'll get some people out of my firm for them. You go to court on June 7th. It's a pretrial hearing."

"What you think gone happen?"

"Well conspiracy's a very hard charge to beat, even in a state court so we are aiming for the best plan we can get unless you feel comfortable taking it to trial."

"This too much right now." I said.

Take your time you still have close to 2 months, your paid up so just stay outta trouble kid and I'll keep you posted on everything pertaining to both cases.

"Bet."

CHAPTER 35

JG

Why was I being taken to federal custody and everybody else were state? I didn't understand! They had me in a room by myself now for hours. I hadn't even got to make a phone call yet. I was wondering about a lot of shit while I was in the room. It was almost an hour before an agent came in to talk to me. "Mr. Gaines, do you understand where you are?"

"I think so but why am I in federal custody?"

"You're being held under federal custody because you're part of an ongoing investigation. Is there anything you wanna say?"

"Just get me to my bunk please."

"Okay, here's our card if you want to talk to us about anything."

"They put me in black and whites and sent me to the federal side. I was hesitant about calling D because I aint know if he had anything to do with this or not, I didn't know nobody else's number. I would have to sit tight and wait on my people to find me!

Darius

A few blocks away, I was leaving the lawyer's office nervous as fuck. I felt like I was being watched from every way I looked. I headed back to the apartment. The furniture truck was pulling off as I pulled up; I walked into the apartment and was astounded. They laid the crib out; they had everything, shit for every room, from the dining room to the bathrooms. They were decorating the bedroom.

"Damn that's a big ass bed."

"It's a Cali-King," Kia said.

"Who all gone be sleeping in that."

"Her and her baby."

"The couch is a pull-out. I'm a sleep in the front when I'm here."

"What you mean when you here?"

"Who gone run the double?" She asked.

"Fuck that double, let his LT run it, I just left from the lawyer office and he told me, they holding bro under federal custody for dope."

"The fed's got him?"

"Yeah, we need to lay low, I'm a send Sue to go see him in the next day or two too see what up. In the meantime you need to find you a job and just lay-low till we see what's going on?"

"Nigga, I aint never had to see "what's going on"!"

"Nigga I aint never had no job." She went on.

"I can probably get you on with me." Susie said.

"Aight but I need to go get my shit from me and Jazz's Condo."

"Sue you cool here by yourself for a while?"

"Yeah, bring something to eat back though,"

"Here order some pizza and wings, we a be back."

"My baby can't eat no pizza and wings."

"I'm a stop on my way back and get some food for the baby," Kia told her as we were on our way out.

I took Kia to her spot out east. It was a nice size place and the inside had the "home" feeling. "Who live here with y'all?" I asked.

"Just me and her, her people own the whole building but I don't wanna stay here by myself."

"How much is the rent."

"It's free to us but I don't know if her folks gone be tripping cause' she aint around."

"Well grab whatever you came to grab so we can get out of here." I looked around while she went to the back.

"D come here I need ya help." When I entered the room she was no were in sight. I looked in the closet and seen her bent over looking into something, her G- string was rising above her waist line and it immediately got my dick hard.

I walked up behind her and grabbed her by the waist. "Um uhn Darius, I know you fucked ya girl earlier when you went home, plus now aint the time. Here hold this open." She passed me a trash bag and began filling it with clothes, shoes and other miscellaneous shit. She then opened a safe that was under the carpet, it was filled with money, jewelry and drugs. I just watched as she grabbed some weed and all the money. "What you gone do with that dope?"

"I'm a leave it here till we figure something out, it's safe here."

"Well lets go."

When we got in the car Drea called me. I asked Kia to be quiet while I answered.

"Hello?"

"What up baby, what you doing?"

"A little running around, tryna get shit together for bro and his people, where you at?"

"I'm bout to pick up Krissy and run around for a bit. Can we spend some time together tonight?"

YYeah, you know you aint gotta ask that."

"Well, I know you had a long day already I wanna take some frustration off of you."

"Ohhh... ah.. yea, we gone do something special."

"Babe, you alright?"

"Yeah, I almost ran into the back of the car in front of me, I'm a call you when I'm on my way home." I lied.

'Okay, be careful, love you!"

"Love you too!"

I hung up the phone and looked at Kia who was acting like she wasn't just playing with my dick while I was on the phone.

"That's what you on?" I grilled her.

"Nah, I'm just a lil spontaneous and wanna see if you can handle 2 bitches at the same time."

"Yeah I can definitely handle that, but that's that funny shit I was talking about. You see the situation I'm in, it's your choice whether you wanna fuck with me like that but if you do you gone play by my rules and rule number 1 is, to respect my relationship with my girl. If you feel like you can't do that we can stop any extra sexual or emotional shit now cause I aint leaving my girl for you or Susie and both of y'all know that! She got in strict compliance cause she know I'm a stand up nigga.

" What you gone do?"

"Nigga I was just testing you, I can handle myself in any situation I'm in."

"You aint making yourself clear Kia."

"I-will-not-get-in-the-way of your little girlfriend Darius, I can play my part. I just want some dick every now and then."

"I can't tell you could of had some already."

"I'm a get it when I want it, I aint no wham-bam- Thank-you-Maam."

"I hear you." She leaned over and kissed me on the cheek and said, "We gone be cool just see me as a friend."

I was tired of driving Susie's Sebring around so against my brother's judgement I pulled up to my house to hop in my Monte. "Grab some food for her baby and I'm a see y'all later."

"Okay, be careful."

"Tell her to try and set up a visit for bro, matter fact you do it for her." "Okay boss man, anything else you want me to do?" she said in a sassy voice.

"Let me get some head before you get out."

"Naw, you got a hot date tonight wouldn't want you to be late for it, bye boy."

I started to say something else, but she took her finger and put it over my lip and hit the automatic unlock button on the door.

CHAPTER 36

The night was still young and I hadn't heard from my bro all day, I was worried about him and missing him. I decided to call the pill man and do some X. I bought two triple X number 1's and went to Hangtime to buy a fit. I picked-out a nice LRG fit and a pair of cool grey Jordans. I went home, popped a pill and took a nice hot shower. By time I got out the shower I was rolling hard as hell. I had to talk to my girl. I called her and she answered on the 3rd ring.

"Hello."

"What up sexy, where you at?"

"Still riding with Krissy."

"When you coming home?"

"I'm close; I'll be there in about 10 minutes."

"Cool, grab some blunts and a fifth." After hanging up, I put in UGKs underground King album (chopped and screwed) and put the TV on Sports center. I lit up a square and by the times it was gone, Drea and Krissy were walking in with a fifth of goose. I grabbed the bottle and told her to roll-up.

"Damn baby, you all fresh and looking good."

"You said you miss me and wanted tonight to be special."

"Well I need to be feeling how you feeling!"

"I gave her the other pill and she swallowed it dry and chased it with the Goose.

"That was strong, let me go get dressed" she said. She went and took a shower while me and Krissy watched the NBA playoffs.

"You know bro locked up don't you."

"Yeah I heard. Sorry to hear that D."

"You gone write him or go see him?"

"That nigga wasn't tryna fuck with me when he was out, but I'm a do what I can for him."

We smoked the rest of the blunt and chilled out for a second. Drea finally came out from the back in some black and gold heels and a black skirt that showed every curve on her body.

"Y'all swear y'all looking good tonight, where y'all going?" Krissy asked. "First, we dropping yo ass off then we just gone get in the wind."

We poured the goose in a water bottle, rolled up 4 more blunts and hopped in the Chevy.

After dropping Krissy off we found ourselves downtown walking on the canal. "This is so relaxing after the long day I had." "Yeah it is but these heels killing me." We sat on the bench for a while and talked about a lot of shit.

"So what you gone do if I gotta do some time for this case?" I asked.

"What you think I'm a do? Leave you? Plus I gotta tell you something?" "What up?"

"I'm pregnant?" I was ecstatic and the X enhanced my feelings.

"For real, how far along are you?"

"Some weeks"

"Is it a boy or a girl?"

"I don't know yet, I haven't been to the doctor, I took a self test."

I hugged her and we kissed on the bench for what felt like 20 minutes.

"You wanna get a room downtown for the night?"

"Yeah we gotta celebrate cause after tonight I aint doing no type of drugs"

"I know you aint, but we having fun tonight."

We got a room at the Hyatt and fucked each other's brains out. After the second round I was done! I had had a long day and it all caught up with me at once. When I woke up it was close to noon, I got up, sparked up a blunt and it instantly kicked my high back in, I looked at Drea and admired her beauty as she slept. I was feeling bad cause I hadn't been spending a lot of time with her but that made me love her more cause she wasn't bugging me about the shit.

I pulled the cover down to expose her bare breast and started sucking on them till she woke up. Once she was up I made my way down her stomach to her diamond belly ring. I continued my journey down to neatly shaven pussy where I inserted my tongue and went to work; it was like her pussy just stayed wet even while she was sleep. By now she was fully alert and her back arched with her long sexy legs pointed to the celling. I ate that pussy till my whole face was glossy and she was begging for me to put it in. I put her legs on my shoulder as I slid up in her, I had no worries at the time and pounded her as she bit on my neck and dug her nails in my back.

"let me hit it from the back" I told her.

She turned over and tooted her ass in the air, I went back in her and crashed her till she was lying on her stomach and moving her hips like a snake. I started speeding up as I felt my nut getting closer and closer she could tell cause' she started grinding super hard.

"Don't come yet, wait on me!" she moaned out.

I was holding my breath trying to give her all I had but couldn't hold it anymore. She was too wet, I bust the biggest nut I ever busted and she must've came too, because she got to moaning and getting even more wet. I rolled over exhausted. "That's how you start ya day off," I said. She rolled over and laid on my chest till we both passed out again. "KNOCK KNOCK KNOCK, room service," was all we heard.

"Hold up." I put on my boxers and shorts and opened the door.

"Would you like your room to be cleaned or something to eat Mr.... "

"Naw we bout to leave but thanks."

The pill had my appetite gone so I sparked up another blunt as we started getting on our clothes and headed out. "Damn, its 5:00 already? We was fucked up last night wasn't we?"

"Yeah, you was a horny lil something."

"I still am."

"You aint had enough yet?"

"It's never enough."

"Come here, she pulled out my dick and sucked it as we rode home. We went in the house, took a shower and I put my same clothes back on while she put on some booty shorts and a beater.

"I'm a be home a lil later, I got some shit I need to take care of."

"Okay, I probably stay in the house and clean up today, so I'm a be here if you need me or want me."

"Don't say it like that I'm a be home later."

I kissed her and bounced. I hopped back in the Chevy and headed up north. I walked in the apartment and they were on the laptop.

"What up with y'all?"

"She filling out her application."

"That's what's up; y'all get the visit shit set up?"

"Yeah I'm a go in the morning at 9:30, Kia gone keep the baby for me." "That's cool, ask him what he need me to do and if he need anything." "I got you!"

CHAPTER 37

JG

"Gaines, you have a visit." I went to the visiting room as is, fuck a line-up and all the shit; I needed to talk to somebody ASAP! I was a little fucked up when I saw Susie sitting in the visit room at the table I was assigned to. "Hey bro." She said sounding sincere.

"What up Susie" I replied back dryly.

"What's up with bro.?"

"He cool, he sent me because he aint want Kia or his self to come down here not knowing what was going on. He told me to ask you want you want him to do for you?"

"Tell him I need him to go to my double, look in the basement under the stairs and clean the safe out. The code is 27-14-11. Tell him to send me a G and put the rest up in case I beat this shit."

"Okay, you said 27-14-11 right?"

"Yeah."

"He told me to give you my number so you can call through me, if you need to. Oh yeah he said do you want him to bond out the crew."

"Not with my money, or his, if they want to get bonded out they should have the money to do so and someone to do it."

"When you go to court?"

"Shiiiit, aint no telling. The feds don't tell you shit they just come and get you one day, could be years."

"Okay, anything else you want me to tell him?"

"Tell him to move smooth. Stay low and I love him. I'm a try to call you soon."

"Alright bro, keep ya head up and call whenever you need to. Kia staying at the spot with me so you can call for her too."

"Aight sis be cool."

I gave her a hug after she wrote down her number then I left. At first I was shitty about seeing Susie but after I thought about it, it might have been the right move, maybe that nigga was a real life player who could control his hoes, I ain't know, but I was damn sure happy it worked out like this.

SUSIE

Leaving the visit I was feeling pretty good about my whole situation. Regardless of the fact that D had a whole other life with the bitch Andrea, I had to respect what he was doing for me. Kia and I were becoming close too, she was like the sister I never had, and she was very helpful with the baby too. I ain't know if Darius was fucking her or not but I could tell it was more than what they made it out to be. They was probably fucking right now but I couldn't trip if he was. She was beautiful and sexy so I know he was attracted to her but I guess it is something I'm gone have to deal with.

CHAPER 38

Summer was flying and it was a couple days before I went to court. Everything had been going just fine. Me an Drea were happy, she was starting to show and I took over her weed operation so the money was coming in. Kia and Susie was working together and getting along just fine. While JG was waiting on a court date, his crew was just sitting in the county waiting on trial dates.

My lawyer had been calling me telling me they wanted me to sign a 10 year plea or be ready for trial. I kept saying go to trial but I was bluffing. I had no intentions on going to trial and it was starting to stress me out a little bit. The day before my court date I was running around like a chicken with no head trying to tie some loose ends. I came home to Drea and she was just nagging about everything. I wanted to just sit back and get fucked up. After getting her what she was crying for all day, I went to the pill man and bought a naked lady triple stack. I rolled up some blunts and just rode around town getting high thinking about the last few years of my life. I was happy but my conscious would kill me sometimes. I had money, a main bitch and two side bitches living together who I knew I could have whenever I wanted one of them. I had become a man in what seemed like overnight.

My main man was in the feds and my lil brother was in Texas in college. I ain't have no niggas out here with me; my bitches had become my niggas! My thoughts were interrupted by my phone ringing. It was Kia, "What up Kia?"

"Why you ain't come see us, we want to have fun with you. We know you go to court tomorrow and hope you not worried about it. But we do wanna spend time with you in case they be on some bullshit."

"Aight, I'll be there in a while." I hung up, and went back to my thoughts. I couldn't believe how my life had turned out. I was cool, I mean I had everything a 22 year old could want but I wasn't happy though. I was still missing something. I stopped at the L before heading to the apartment. I bought a fifth of Patron and was wasted by the time I walked in the apartment. The lights were all off and it was fairly quiet besides the slow jam mix tape that could be heard from the back, I made my way to the bedroom where the music was coming from and was turned on when I saw Kia's head between Susie legs.

"Y'all gone party without me?" I said in a slurry voice.

"Naw come on and join us." Kia said as she lifted her ass up in the air.

I dropped my shorts and slid in her raw; she felt like a virgin but took every inch as I slit it in her slowly. The deeper I put it in the wetter she got. The wetter she got the more aggressive she got with Susie. I had her cumming in no time. "Let's switch positions." Susie said. They put me on my back As Susie straddled my face, I played with her titties while Kia sucked my dick. She stopped for a minute as I continue to slurp away on Susie's clit… "Bang! Bang!" was all I heard before Susie's limp body fell on me. I looked up and saw Kia standing there naked holding what looked like a desert eagle.

"What the fuck you kill her for Kia? You thought she was gone get us fucked up or something?"

"Nah, I don't leave witnesses."

"What the fuck you talking about?"

"Nigga Tori was my cousin, I told you all I wanted from you was some dick but I guess I'll help myself to everything I can. "BOC, BOC, BOC," was all I heard before seeing the light!

TO BE CONTINUED...

About the Author

Corey L Jackson is 31 years old and lives in INDPLS, IN with his son.

He enjoys Music, Sports and spending time with his family.

Follow him on Facebook and Instagram @ Corey Jackson or @Coreyjthewriter.

www.ingramcontent.com/pod-product-compliance
Lightning Source LLC
Chambersburg PA
CBHW010248270626

47156CB00023B/2985
9780578190822